OUT OF THE DARK

BOOKS BY
WELWYN WILTON KATZ

TIME GHOST
COME LIKE SHADOWS
WHALESINGER
THE THIRD MAGIC
FALSE FACE
WITCHERY HILL
SUN GOD, MOON WITCH
THE PROPHECY OF TAU RIDOO

OUT OF THE DARK

WELWYN WILTON KATZ

A GROUNDWOOD BOOK

Douglas & McIntyre   Vancouver / Toronto

Groundwood Books / Douglas & McIntyre Ltd.
585 Bloor Street West
Toronto, Ontario M6G 1K5

The publisher gratefully acknowledges the assistance of the
Canada Council and the Ontario Arts Council.

Canadian Cataloguing in Publication Data

Katz, Welwyn
Out of the dark

"A Groundwood book".
ISBN 0-88899-262-9
ISBN 0-88899-241-6 (trade format)

I. Title.

PS8571.A889087 1995   jC813'.54   C95-931078-9
PZ7.K37Ou 1995

Design by Michael Solomon
Cover art and text decoration by Martin Springett
Maps by Doug Bale
Printed and bound in Canada

ACKNOWLEDGEMENTS

Thanks to the Canada Council for the grant that made it possible for me to do my research in Newfoundland, and to write this book. Thanks also to David Adams and Sophie Bessey of the Tickle Inn, Ship Cove, Newfoundland, for answering my many questions; to Clayton Colbourne and Dwayne Goudie and all the other helpful guides at L'Anse aux Meadows; to Sherry Campbell and Calmond Beaufield at Pistolet Bay Provincial Park; to Ian, Meghan and Lizzie Stewart, who wandered the bog with us and identified wildflowers and were endlessly helpful with the on-site research, and to Kerry, who wasn't there but wished she had been; and to the friendly children of Ship Cove: Tanya Hurley, Melissa Hurley, Shannon Tucker, Lorne Hedderson and Tara Regular. I'm also grateful to Jim Freedman and to Mike Spence of the Anthropology Department of the University of Western Ontario, and to Bob McGhee of the Museum of Civilization in Ottawa. My deep thanks as well to Alice Walsh, a fine novelist who was lucky enough to grow up on the Northern Peninsula and kind enough to read my first draft to correct the mistakes I had made because I hadn't grown up there myself. I am also most sincerely grateful to my friend Catharine Leggett, who put me on the right path when the plot had gone astray. Last—never least—thanks to Meredith for being my second set of eyes, and for suggesting the perfect place for my book's Viking house and its lookout point; and to Doug for his endless practical help, creative suggestions, and his indispensable and unswerving support

This book is for Joan and Mel and Katie and Elizabeth, who gave me my first real taste of L'Anse aux Meadows, a taste that made me plot the book—and go.

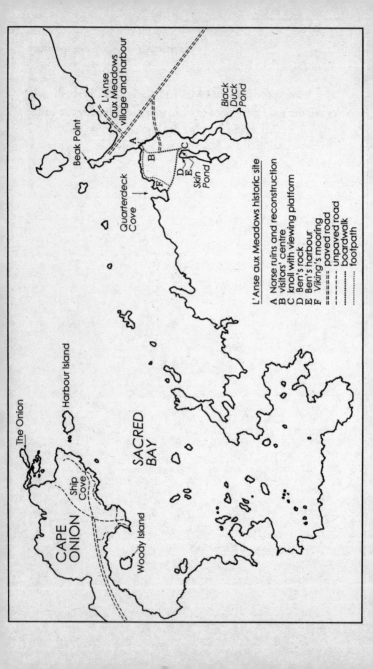

The Onion

Harbour Island

CAPE ONION

Ship Cove

Woody Island

SACRED BAY

Beak Point

L'Anse aux Meadows village and harbour

A

B

F

Quarterdeck Cove

D

E

C

Skin Pond

Black Duck Pond

L'Anse aux Meadows historic site

A Norse ruins and reconstruction
B visitors' centre
C knoll with viewing platform
D Ben's rock
E Ben's harbour
F Viking's mooring

═══════ paved road
─────── unpaved road
········· boardwalk
─ ─ ─ ─ footpath

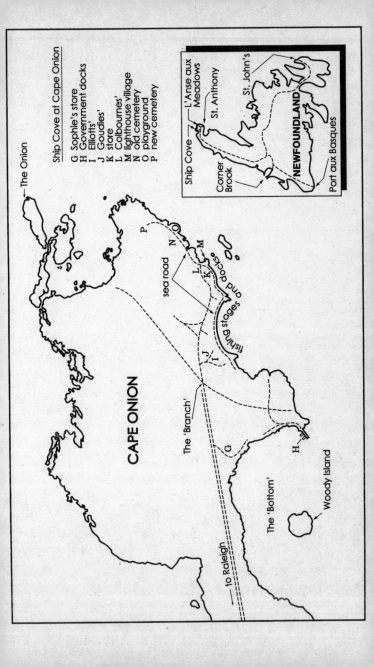

The Onion

Ship Cove at Cape Onion

G Sophie's store
H Government docks
I Elliotts'
J Goudies',
K store
L Colbournes'
M lighthouse village
N old cemetery
O playground
P new cemetery

CAPE ONION

The 'Branch'

sea road

fishing stages and docks

to Raleigh

The 'Bottom'

G

H

Woody Island

NEWFOUNDLAND

Ship Cove
L'Anse aux Meadows
St. Anthony
St. John's
Corner Brook
Port aux Basques

ONE

The seal wasn't pure white, so it couldn't be a baby. But still it had that soft, trusting look that baby seals have on TV, just before somebody batters them to death for their pelts. Its big eyes looked up at Ben as if he were something that ought to be important, only it couldn't remember why. Ben knelt on the sharp beach rocks in front of it. It was not much bigger than his little brother Keith.

The cold Newfoundland wind blew salt spray into Ben's face. He squinted through it at the seal that had dragged itself ashore. It was not a place he would have chosen for refuge, if he had been a seal. This beach might be a decent haven in another wind, but today the surf crashed into the bay. For safety the little seal had had to flipper itself halfway up to the overhanging sod edge of the lands above the shore, and even here the water splashed it. There was nowhere for it to hide. Above this place, amid rolling leagues of treeless, boggy grassland, the only safe places were man-made and not for seals: reproduction Viking houses made of sod, the visitors' centre, cars and trucks in a parking lot. None of these would be of any use to a seal seeking a peaceful place to die.

There were drops of red on the beach stones. Ben was pretty sure there was a whole pool of it under the seal's body.

The Vikings had hunted seals. They would never feel sick, looking at a dying one. Ben made himself regard the seal stolidly.

Tor was a hunter, a provider. Karlsefni relied on him as much for this as for his shipbuilder's hands. He had not been named after the thunder god for nothing.

"There'll be good meat on this one, Tor," Karlsefni approved. "And warm fur for the lady Gudrid's bed. Your spear aims well."

Ben blinked. It couldn't have been a spear that had injured this seal. Not nowadays. Sharks, maybe. Or killer whales. Ben hoped it wasn't humans. He hoped there hadn't been a gun.

It had been a spear that had begun the first war of the gods. Odin One-Eye, father of the gods of Asgard, had cast his spear at the leader of the gods that dwelt in the Upper Air, and soon the towering wall around Asgard was in ruins. The wall was eventually rebuilt by a stone giant who demanded the goddess Freya as his wife, but Loki the Trickster saved her. It was one of Tor's favourite stories, told and retold over the longhouse fire in the depths of winter, when snow made iron of the ground and men needed tales of Freya's pools of golden tears to remind them of spring.

Mom's bedtime stories had often been about the Norse gods like Odin and Thor and the giants and monsters they defeated, or about real Vikings like Karlsefni, the first European settler of North America. Ben loved the stories. He loved most things about the adventurous Norsemen who had fought and traded and stolen their way all over the world. He spent half his spare time drawing pictures of them, and when he'd been younger, he'd often played Vikings with his friends

Kevin and Peter. But they hadn't really understood about the Vikings. Kevin loved their looting and raiding and Peter loved their dangerous exploration of an ocean covered horizon to horizon with jagged shards of ice. But shipbuilding, climbing cliffs for puffin eggs, or meeting together in the first real parliament in Europe left them both cold.

When they played Vikings, Peter and Kevin always wanted to be the big-name heroes: Leif the Lucky, who came to the New World, built some sod huts and left again; or Eric the Red, who discovered Greenland, but never even saw North America. Ben was different. He wasn't interested in big names. He was always Tor, Karlsefni's man, shipbuilder and explorer of the New World. Ben didn't know if there had been a real Tor with Karlsefni's expedition, but it didn't matter. Tor was a good name.

Peter and Kevin eventually got bored with the Viking game, so Ben played it only when he was alone. He stopped that, too, eventually. But now and then Tor came back to him. A dying seal on a Newfoundland beach, and Tor was with him.

It made sense, of course. If Tor belonged anywhere, it was here in L'Anse aux Meadows, the only proven Viking settlement in North America. Leif the Lucky had come here, and then his brother Thorvald and finally Karlsefni, coming to settle this new land with his wife Gudrid and the most loyal of his men. If there had been a Tor, he would have come with Karlsefni. Tor would have been here, where Ben now was.

Dad and Mom had met on this very beach, years ago, on the archaeological dig. Mom had come to L'Anse aux Meadows to help her father excavate the Viking remains. She had been barely sixteen, but people accepted her because her father was the famous archaeologist Evan Torland. Dad had been a high-school kid, one of the two Elliott boys who lived across the bay in Ship Cove. Grandpa had hired both Dave and Lorne Elliott to help dig. By the time the summer was over, Lorne was working full-time with Frances, helping to clean and catalogue the finds. Lorne found out Frances loved carving wood and making figures out of clay. Frances found out Lorne loved to write. Later, they found out they loved each other.

"A happily-ever-after ending to a fairy-tale romance," Mom had said, when she'd told Ben the story for the first time. She had laughed when Ben had replied, "But you like Viking stories, Mom, not fairy-tales!"

Even as a five-year-old, he had known the difference. In Viking stories mistletoe was not just a pretty plant to kiss under, but the thing that killed the beloved god Balder and helped bring about Ragnarok, the end of the world.

Mom and Dad had always said they would take the boys to L'Anse aux Meadows to see the Viking settlement where they had met. But Mom's regular job didn't earn much, and she usually spent every extra penny on wood for her carvings. Dad was firm about putting away anything left out of his writing income in case the next book didn't sell. There never seemed to be enough money for a family vacation.

But then, two years ago they had driven to Florida to stay with Grandpa in his condominium.

It was logical to choose Florida over Newfoundland. Grandpa needed company. And he was getting old. Another year, his arthritis might be too bad to let him take them to Disneyworld as he had promised. And of course there was no Disneyworld in Newfoundland. Even Ben had thought that the Vikings could wait for a visit till another year.

Now it *was* another year and they were in Newfoundland, but it wasn't just for a visit. Not two days ago they had actually moved here, moved away from Ottawa to Ship Cove, where Dad had grown up. And Mom wasn't with them.

A wild wind on the bay today, but offshore for once, safe. Tor knew that, though it was his art to help build ships, not to sail them. He was the son of a master shipbuilder in Iceland and had carved since he was old enough to hold a knife. There was no one among Karlsefni's men could shape wood for a skiff or a knarr as Tor could. But for steering a ship or setting its sails to get the most from a crosswind, there was none better than Ulf. He was a big, round-shouldered man with huge hands and a gentle smile that had misled more enemies in battle than Tor could count. He was smiling now, leaning on the knarr's steering oar.

"Haul that sail," Ulf called, and Tor did as he was told. The little vessel moved faster.

Rollo leaned out over the scrollboards in the bow, pointing and cheering. The wind carried his words back to them. "There it is! Leifsbudir!"

Tor saw the settlement at the same moment, eight houses of wood and sod humped against the grasslands, smoke rising from the holes in the roofs. The women would be serving the meal in the main longhouse by now, not expecting the hunting expedition back until tomorrow at the earliest. But the settlement would not suffer from their early return. There was a huge heap of seal meat on the bottomboards of the knarr and dozens of skins hanging from toggles, ready for tanning.

The seal twitched suddenly, its body tightening. A lot of blood. Yes. Ben began to reach out a hand, but caught himself. There was nothing he could do. Even as he watched, the seal's eyes went dim and out of focus. Ben knew what that meant.

"Ben!" Keith's voice called shrilly from farther up the beach. "Dad's looking for you! We're going home in a few minutes. Hey, Ben!"

Ben got slowly to his feet. For one moment more he

blinked down at the seal. Its eyes had already filmed over. "I'm sorry," Ben said to it, or to himself, he didn't really know. Animals died. People died. There was nothing anyone could do. He made himself start toward his brother.

"What were you looking at?" Keith said, moving forward.

"Nothing." Ben took larger steps, blocking his little brother's view of the beach.

"Looks like a heap of rags," Keith said, peering round him.

"I said it was nothing. Where's Dad?"

Keith turned, pointing to the biggest of the sod buildings behind the woven wood fence. "In the longhouse, looking for you. He bet me you'd be there. Guess I won the bet, huh?" He grinned triumphantly.

"I was in the longhouse for quite a while," Ben said.

The original longhouse and its outbuildings had been farther up the meadow near the brook, but after nine centuries of wind and weather, the walls and grass roofs had tumbled down until only low ridges remained. Parks Canada had built the reproduction along with a couple of smaller huts to show the tourists what the real thing had been like.

Ben couldn't deny that the reproduction settlement looked great. Inside the longhouse a couple of tiny fires made more smoke than light on the open hearths in the centre, and the only natural light came from the smoke-holes in the roof and the two low doors. The built-in sleeping platforms covered with furs and the private room at the front were nice. Ben had tried hard to imagine Karlsefni and his lady Gudrid sitting there, going over the day's activities: how many fish the men had brought in, who the women were gossiping about, what the hostile Skraeling natives were up to. But the whole time he was there, the guides went on about bog-iron and forges and how many wooden artifacts they had found on what site and why they knew they were artifacts and not just ordinary bits of bog-preserved driftwood. It all made it hard for Ben to imagine he was really in Viking times.

Afterward he had gone outside into the cold, grey day and taken the boardwalk to the ridges that marked the real Viking houses. He'd bent over and touched them and stepped into the centre of their outlines one after the other—eight of them in all. He was alone out there. Nobody else had braved the cold and the wind to see where the Vikings had actually lived, hung their fish to dry, mended their ships and manned their palisade to keep out the hostile Skraelings. Ben didn't think even Dad had spent any time here, though twenty years ago he'd helped dig up these ridges. He was too busy poring over the displays in the visitors' centre up the hill. And now he, like everyone else, was in the imitation longhouse, while the real one was as unattended as it had been for the ten centuries before the archaeologists discovered it.

"Did you see the furs on the bed?" Keith asked, leading the way to the gate in the wooden fence surrounding the reproduction settlement. "I bet Leif the Lucky skinned them himself."

Keith was no different than all the other tourists, oohing over the fake settlement while the real thing lay there, unnoticed. It made Ben angry, suddenly. He caught up to his brother. "Leif the Lucky didn't skin a single one of those furs. Didn't you pay any attention to that movie in the visitors' centre? You deaf, or just dumb?"

"I'm not dumb," Keith shot back, stopping in his tracks. "The guide said the biggest house in the settlement would have belonged to Leif the Lucky." He gestured at the longhouse. "Anybody can see this is the biggest house. And if it's Leif's house, why couldn't he have skinned those furs?"

"Because none of the furs are more than twenty years old. And this isn't the real longhouse. You really are dumb, aren't you?"

"If anybody's dumb," Keith flared, "it's you." He sputtered for a moment, then added triumphantly, "At least *I* don't call a bunch of ordinary kids *Skraelings*."

"What are you talking about?"

"This morning, in Ship Cove, when we were getting milk at that store. You said those boys buying candy were Skraelings."

Trust Keith to overhear, Ben thought. I only whispered it.

"They weren't even Indians," Keith went on. "In Mom's stories the Skraelings were Indians."

"First Nations," Ben corrected automatically.

"Well, those boys in the store weren't. They were just like you and me."

"What I meant," Ben said, "was that the *Vikings* would have called them Skraelings." He put his hands in his pockets. "Those boys lived here before us, see? Just like the Skraelings, when the Vikings came. And the Skraelings didn't like the Vikings, and those boys didn't like us."

"How do you know?"

"Anybody could see that from the way they looked at us."

"You walked away before they could even say hi."

"They didn't want to say hi."

"How do you know?" Keith said again, but this time he sounded honestly bewildered. Ben just looked at him. Keith was only a kid. He hadn't figured things out yet. He didn't understand things the way a thirteen-year-old did: that most people didn't like newcomers; that you had better watch out, if you were unlucky enough to be one.

"I will lend you my houses in the New World," Leif told Karlsefni while Tor stood silently by, watching the lords at feast. "Leifsbudir will keep you safe in the first years of your settlement."

"From storms, perhaps," Karlsefni said. "The Skraelings may be more difficult."

"So Thorvald my brother discovered," Leif agreed. He raised his cup, and Karlsefni's wife Gudrid hurried to fill it. "But the timber, man, the timber is worth a battle or two. And what Skraeling can harm a Viking, if that Viking is ready for him?"

"There's Dad," Keith said. He ran through the gate toward an upturned boat that lay on two sawhorses beside the longhouse. "Hey, Dad!"

Lorne Elliott was a tall man, and rather too thin. His face, especially, seemed dominated by bones. He had a generous mouth, but his eyes were private, deepset and very dark and thoughtful. Once when Ben was little he had drawn a picture of his father. He had worked hard at it, and when he was finished he took his thickest, blackest crayon and drew a circle around it. Sometimes, even now, he thought of his father as having that circle around him.

Mom had been different, small and fair and quick. Ben had tried dozens of times to get her image down on paper, but sometimes she was beautiful and sometimes she was plain; she could look strong and beaky or fragile as a flower. In the end he had decided that she was not one image, any more than she was one colour.

It was her hands he liked the most, small and white with clever, stubby fingers, very steady. Sometimes he would wake at night thinking he felt them resting gently on his own, the way they had guided him when he was little with paintbrush, knife, and finally the woodcarver's chisel. And then came the day he had carved something entirely on his own. A boat, it had been. She'd stared at it a long time, and then she'd nodded, a hard, decisive nod, utterly professional. From then on she hadn't guided him. Instead they'd worked together on things, each of them helping the other.

Dad and Keith were waiting for him. Ben quickened his steps. "Cold on the beach?" Dad asked.

"I guess," Ben said. "For July."

"I was sure you'd be in the longhouse. There's a fire in there."

"I'm going back in." Keith stuck his chin out at Ben. "I've gotta ask that guide something." He was gone before his father could reply.

"Did you go in at all?" Dad asked Ben.

"Sure I did."

"Didn't you like it?"

"It'd be better if they let us be in there alone."

"I like it better than I expected to," his father said. "Even with the guides and all the tourists, when I was squatting in front of that fire I found myself imagining I was Leif Eiriksson, with Tyrkir the German nagging at me on one side and someone else cursing on the other because they'd dropped the meat in the fire."

Surprise kept Ben silent for a moment. Dad, imagining he was a Viking, too. For a moment he was almost tempted to tell him about Tor. But Ben had never even told his mother about Tor, and the Vikings were always more Mom's than anybody else's.

"Are you going to write a book about this place?" Ben asked suddenly.

"I've been thinking about it."

"What'll it be about?"

His father's face smoothed over. "Not sure yet."

Even if he had been sure, he wouldn't have said. Dad never talked about his writing. It was something private, something he did inside himself over the computer or staring out a window into the late-night darkness, not hearing the boys ask him questions, not knowing they were even still awake.

"I hope Keith's not going to take all day in there," Dad said, suddenly impatient. "We've got a lot of boxes to unpack at home."

Home. A word that didn't feel right. That purple and pink cottage across the bay didn't feel right, either. Bare wood floors and unpacked boxes, the table and chairs that belonged in the kitchen in their house in Ottawa now sitting beside a window that looked out on a cold Viking sea …

His father was watching him closely. "Ben, I hope you're going to give Ship Cove a chance."

Ben took his hands out of his pockets and examined a bit of string he'd found there. "The thing is," he said to the string, "I don't know why we had to move here."

"It's where I grew up. We have…connections here."

Ben wound the string around his thumb. "Grandpa and Grandma Elliott are both dead. Aunt Ellie moved to Toronto. Uncle Dave's—"

"— in St. John's. I do know all that, Ben."

Ben looked up from the string. "So what do you mean, *connections*?" He couldn't keep the hostility out of his voice.

"Family isn't the only thing that can connect you to a place —although I might remind you I've got at least a dozen second and third cousins scattered between here and St. Anthony."

"You don't know any of them. You haven't seen them since you were a kid."

"That isn't the point. I'm a Newfoundlander. I belong in Ship Cove. All the years I was away, part of me was still here on the edge of the sea." He paused. "And especially these days, Ben, there's a quiet here that I need. I really need it."

What about what I need? Ben thought. What about me? I'm from Ontario, not here. I belong in Ottawa, a big city. I don't belong in Ship Cove, where there's only about two hundred people and strangers stick out like a sore thumb. He stared angrily at his dad.

"I know it's a small place," his father said quietly. "It'll be quite an adjustment, after Ottawa. But half of you is a

Newfoundlander, Ben. And you haven't been all that happy in Ottawa this last while, have you?" Ben was silent. "Anyway, you like the Vikings," his father went on. "You've always liked them."

"They're gone now," Ben said. "And when they were here, they were on this side of the bay, not over there in Ship Cove."

"Nobody's ever really gone from a place, if they've once lived there," Lorne said very quietly. "And even though we'll be living in Ship Cove, if I'm going to set the next book in L'Anse aux Meadows, I'll be over here a lot. You can come with me whenever you like. Maybe next time we'll come by boat."

"We don't have a boat."

"Not yet. But we will. Can't live on the edge of the ocean and not have an outboard and engine." His voice as he said that sounded as foreign as the woman in the store this morning who'd called everybody "my dear" and wouldn't let Dad get out with the milk for almost half an hour. But then he went on, and he sounded normal again. "I've asked Ed Jefferson to look out for a boat for us."

"Not the same guy who got us the house?" Ben made a face. "I hope the boat won't be pink and purple."

His father smiled a little. "Newfoundlanders take their boats more seriously than their houses. You'll like having a boat, Ben. I was out in my dad's by myself when I was younger than you, tootling all over the bay."

Ben did like boats. He wandered over to the one upturned on sawhorses near the entrance of the sod house. It was only a skiff, not a large Viking knarr of the kind that had brought explorers and settlers from Iceland, but Ben had never seen as beautiful a curve as the one the keel made. He ran one hand along the arc of the bow. It made a continuous sweep, though the weatherbeaten grey planks overlapped. The wood felt alive under his fingers.

His father joined him. "The Vikings came in a boat like this," he murmured.

"Bigger," Ben said. "And with a sail."

"But like this."

"Yes."

They smiled at each other, for once in perfect understanding.

TWO

Ben leaned against his windowsill, staring into the night. It was cold and very late, but he was too restless to stay in bed. Instead he huddled into a blanket and strained his eyes into the darkness outside the salt-streaked glass. He couldn't see a thing. There were a few streetlights in Ship Cove—orange beams that Dad said were good in fog—but from Ben's window none of these could be seen. Nothing at all was visible: not the dandelion jungle between their house and the edge of the hill; not the fishing shacks and docks that lined the bay at the bottom; not the heaving grey sea whose rumbling sigh he could hear even through the glass; not a hint of stars, let alone the sky.

"Fog coming," Dad had said when they'd stopped unpacking boxes that evening. When Ben had looked out the back window, the Goudies' house up the lane had disappeared into swirling eddies of white. There were no other close neighbours. They were alone, an island in a sea of cotton wool.

Dad and Keith seemed to think it was fun. Dad had started a fire in the woodstove and made a big jug of hot chocolate. It had chased the damp away. But Ben could still picture the fog, a tentacled ghost surrounding them in the night.

There had been only a little fog that evening in Florida. Mostly just cotton-candy clouds floating in wisps, though here and there the dips in the road were too thick to see through. Ben had laughed as they drove blindly into them and out again. There was hardly another car on the highway. "A little cold and a little damp and these spoiled Floridians are off shivering to their beds," Mom had declared gaily, pulling into the deserted parking lot at the drugstore.

It hadn't been very late, either. Still light enough to read. "I want to finish my book," Ben had told Mom when she'd asked him to go into the drugstore with her. Drugstores were boring. And Grandpa's prescriptions were never ready when the druggist said they would be.

Gudrid was grinding herbs. She was kneeling as close to the fire as she could, though despite the dank weather outside, the longhouse was warm. The hearth-fires were burning well and for a miracle most of the smoke was actually escaping through the smoke-holes in the roof. It was for light that Gudrid sought the fire, not warmth. She was concentrating hard on the seeds she was grinding in the mortar, leaning into the task, her brow furrowed, a fine line of perspiration on her upper lip. Tor watched her, thinking of his mother, who had ground herbs in just that same way back in Iceland.

At last Gudrid wiped her forehead and sat back on her heels. Tor leaned forward to look in the mortar but drew back hastily, making a face. The paste had a powerful odour.

"Angelica," Gudrid said. She smiled. "The next time you have a nervous headache or disturbance of the stomach, I shall dose you with a tea of this."

"You'll have to catch me first," Tor said.

"That I could do easily, even like this," she teased, indicating her stomach, big with Karlsefni's child.

Tor had been with Karlsefni for five years, ever since he became a man of thirteen. After his lord and lady were wed, he had become Gudrid's man as well as Karlsefni's. He liked her better than any woman he had ever known. He thought she was wise. Sometimes Gudrid seemed to know things—like the time she'd told Tor a whale would come ashore to replenish their food stores, and not a day later, it had.

"This bowl will not stand flat," Gudrid said, showing it to Tor.

He took the wooden bowl from her, then fetched his tools. The slave Unas was on her knees grinding barley nearby. She could usually be counted on for a smile, but today she only grunted at him, sweating as she turned the handle of the quern. Back home the women would make the children take turns at the quern, but here there were no children to help with the women's work. There were men—lots of men—but men did not grind grain. For two days now they had been prevented by fog from hunting and fishing, and most of them were lazing indoors, playing at dice or snoring on their sleeping platforms. Though how anyone could sleep amid all the noise and activity, Tor didn't know.

He had not spent so much time in the busy atmosphere of the longhouse since he was a lad playing with the other boys, stealing curds and tormenting the dogs and skipping out of their mothers' sight whenever chores needed to be done. He smiled to himself, bending over the bowl. It was good to be here, good to smell Freyda's bread baking and hear the thump, thump, thump of Astrid's churn, good to have a job to do for his lady until his lord Karlsefni needed him.

Ben shivered, pulling the blanket closer. The fog crowded the window. He didn't think he had ever been in a house so quiet. He didn't like it. He didn't like anything about this house. It was drafty and damp and the woodstove heated only the big front room properly. His room was painted a horrible green and had no baseboards. Keith's had no doorframe. Nothing was finished. The water came out of the taps smelling of rotten eggs. You had to be careful not to flush the toilet too often because of the septic tank. And there were weird names for things. The pantry was a "back house." The front porch was the "bridge." Dad knew all the names, of course. He had been born in Ship Cove.

Ben and Keith were outsiders, though. Dad couldn't see that. He said they were half Newfoundlanders, but no one here would notice it. Anyway, Ben didn't feel as if he was half a Newfoundlander. He felt like somebody who'd landed on an alien planet.

He didn't belong here. Even the licence plate on their car announced it. *Ontario*, it proclaimed, proudly blue and white.

"It's how they knew you were tourists," the policeman in Florida had said.

It was one of the ways they'd know it here, too.

◆

Dad drew a rough map of Ship Cove at breakfast the next morning. "This is called the Branch," he said, pointing to the place where the paved highway from Raleigh split into three separate dirt roads. He smiled a little ruefully. "No other paved roads in the whole village. I must say I'm a bit worried about the car."

Ben could see why. Coming back from the Viking settlement before supper yesterday Dad had kept their old car to a crawl, but even so the gravel had spun up, and the potholes felt like craters. Most people here seemed to have pickups. But on a single writer's income, it would be a long time before they could afford a new vehicle.

Through a mouthful of toast Keith said, "Maybe if you drive fast enough you'll skip over the potholes."

"We'd only just land in another one," Dad said with a laugh.

"Where are we on this map?" Ben asked. "Our house, I mean."

"Just about here," Dad said, pointing to a thin line he'd sketched downward from the middle road leading from the Branch. He put an X on the map. "That's us." Another X, smaller, closer to the main road. "That's the Goudies'." Their only near neighbours, who had brought them a pot of chowder on their first night. "You can't get lost, though. Just ask anyone, and they'll point you toward home."

"We won't need to ask," Ben said. "All we have to do is look for a blinding glare of pink and purple." He made himself grin. "Joke, Dad, joke."

His father looked at him, then turned pointedly back to his map. "The old harbour is directly down the hill from us, see? On the sea road. Turn right and eventually you'll end up at the government docks—if you don't mind scrambling. The road got washed out a few years ago. The other way, the sea road dead ends at the cemetery on the headland here."

A cemetery, Ben thought. That really was a dead end. He thought of saying it aloud to make Keith laugh. But somehow he didn't feel like it. He looked at Dad's map again. Every road in Ship Cove was the same, a thin dirt line leading nowhere. Couldn't Dad see it? What were they doing here, anyway?

"Cape Onion," Keith read, dripping jam on a corner of the map. "Cool name."

"There's another headland farther west." Lorne pointed again. "It's a great place to look for whales, because you're really high up."

"What kind of whales?" Ben asked, trying hard because his father sounded so eager.

"Humpbacks, mostly, some fin whales. If you're really

lucky you'll see one of them wallowing in the waves, but mostly you just catch sight of their spouts, or their flukes when they dive. I always used to hope I'd hear them sing."

"How do we get there?"

"Over the first headland. Just follow the sea. One thing about Ship Cove. You can never lose track of the sea."

"Except in a fog," Ben pointed out. "Last night, for instance. Or today."

His father laughed. "Today's not real fog, boy. A bit misky, maybe. That's *misty*, to the tourists." He laughed again happily, then went over to the window and looked out. When he went on his voice had the same foreignness it had had yesterday when he'd talked about the boat they were going to buy. "When it's really foggy, foggy enough that you can just about taste it, well, then what we say is, we says it's bank weather. Or capelin weather, sometimes. Capelin's a kind of fish, small, like a sardine." His accent was growing stronger with every word.

"Speak English, Dad," Ben said.

His father turned, blinking at him. "My Newfie roots showing, were they?"

"Will we be going back to L'Anse aux Meadows today?" Ben asked quickly.

Lorne shook his head, frowning a little. "I've got my office to set up. We went there first thing because you both love the Vikings so much and because—" He broke off. "Well, I wanted to see the place again. But it's Ship Cove we live in, not L'Anse aux Meadows."

I *know* that, Ben told himself.

Lorne went on, "When I've finished hooking up the computer and figured out where my books should go, well, then there's the rest of the stuff in the kitchen. And after that there'll be people to meet, maybe even some old friends ..."

"You're glad to be back, aren't you, Dad?" Keith asked, putting a sticky hand on his father's arm.

"Yes, Keith, I am glad. I grew up here. It was hard for me to leave. I guess it's always hard to leave your home." He glanced quickly at Ben before turning back to Keith. "And, yes, I know Ottawa was *your* home. But you're a lot younger than I was. You'll adapt. I don't know that I ever really did."

Ben looked down. Ottawa was where Dad had married Mom, and where Ben and Keith had been born. Ottawa was where all Dad's books had been written. Ottawa was *important*. How could Dad suddenly start acting as if it hadn't ever been that for him?

"You will like it here," Dad said determinedly. "I know you will. It's a kid's paradise. You just have to give it a chance."

Ben looked up. "There aren't any bookstores," he said a little too loudly. "There isn't a library. You can't go out to a movie. There isn't even a restaurant. And there are only two stores in the whole place—and they mostly just sell groceries."

"You'll have access to the school library for ten months of the year," his father said. "We can mail-order books the rest of the time. As for stores, well, there's a mall in St. Anthony, and a library too."

Forty minutes away, Ben thought gloomily.

"At least we can rent videos," Keith put in helpfully. "I saw a lot of them up at the store where we bought the milk yesterday."

Ben had seen them too. *Friday the Thirteenth*, *Alien*, *Nightmare on Elm Street*. And for the kiddies, *Aladdin* and *The Little Mermaid*. Just what he'd always wanted. He picked up the map and pushed back his chair. "Think I'll go out for a while," he said as casually as he could manage.

"That's the way," his father replied, though his eyes were anxious. "Explore, find your bearings, make some friends.

You're bound to meet some kids if you stay on the beach long enough. Or go to one of the stores. That's what we always used to do in the summer. Spear flatfish, throw a line over the wharf and catch sculpins, ride our bikes along the water, get sick on penny candy. It was great. Why don't you take Keith with you?"

Ben shut the door behind him, suddenly in too much of a hurry even to grab for his jacket. Keith could come if he wanted, but Ben wasn't going to hang around and wait for him. Not in that house, with its bright, ugly colours and Keith being so darned cheerful and Dad going on and on about how wonderful it all was. He squared his shoulders and marched deliberately to the edge of the hill overlooking the sea.

It was very cold outside, and very grey. The mist that remained from last night's pea-souper felt like wet gauze. Weeds and rank grasses dripped all around him. The breeze off the North Atlantic had a salty smell with a not-unpleasant edge of seaweed or fish. Over the roofs of the weatherbeaten fishing shacks the sea was the same grey as the sky, with no obvious boundary. Something greenish and small floated fuzzily out there. It might be a bird or a whale. You couldn't tell, without a horizon to give it perspective. It might even be an iceberg.

They had seen icebergs in the Strait of Belle Isle, when they'd been driving up here the day before yesterday. Ben had tried to memorize the shapes and colours, so that when he found his paints and sketchbook again, he could get the memory down on paper. But now that he had unpacked his paints, he had no desire to use them. Those translucent green ice-towers of a few days ago seemed almost as distant to him as Ottawa.

For a while Ben didn't let himself look at the brightly coloured houses below him, in case any of those kids he had seen yesterday were there. He still remembered the inspection they had given him and Keith. The girls had been digging each other in the ribs and giggling, but Ben didn't expect much else from girls. It was the boys that bothered him. There were only three of them, but they'd stood there as if they owned the place, lips pursed and legs planted wide—real tough-guy stuff, showing the interlopers who belonged here and who didn't.

Skraelings.

Tor brought the news to Karlsefni, who was still eating his morning meal. "Twenty or thirty of them," he announced. "Not hostile, so far. They have furs."

"To trade?"

"I think so. One of them—the biggest—kept showing me his pile of furs, then pointing to my axe."

"They want weapons?" Karlsefni demanded incredulously. He threw his head back and laughed. "After what they did to Thorvald Eiriksson, they think we will give them weapons?"

"They already have weapons," Gudrid murmured, refilling her lord's bowl. "How else did Thorvald die?"

"That was luck, no more," Karlsefni said derisively. "Skraeling weapons are inferior. Wood and stone, not iron."

"But there are many of them," Gudrid said very softly. "Many Skraelings, many weapons. And we are few."

"Sixty to their thirty," Tor couldn't help pointing out.

"We are sixty in all of Vinland," Gudrid said, regarding him disapprovingly. "They are thirty in this place alone."

"There is a leader, you say?" Karlsefni demanded of Tor.

"Maybe that biggest one," Tor answered.

"The one who wanted your axe. Yes, yes, wife, what is it?"

Gudrid waited a moment, her head bowed. "It is only that a man might want Tor's axe for many things. It need not be only a weapon."

"It is a good axe," Tor said stiffly. It was his shipbuilding axe, honed to perfection and balanced for his hand. He would never have used it as a weapon.

Astrid had been looking out, twirling her braid. "The biggest Skraeling is handsome," she said, turning and dropping the skin that covered the doorway so that the longhouse immediately darkened.

"We will need the Skraelings' furs, come winter," Gudrid said tentatively. "Could we not teach them something in exchange? Perhaps Tor could show them how to build boats like ours. Theirs are only of skin, and small, Thorvald's men said. They cannot cross oceans in them."

"But we do not want the Skraelings to cross oceans," Karlsefni replied, smiling faintly. "Nevertheless you are right, lady. We should have the furs. Not in trade for knowledge or weapons, however. There will be other things the Skraelings will take. Savages will always give away something useful in exchange for something new to them."

There were no boats out at sea. Ben knew the fishery had been closed a few years before. It was because the fish stocks had been depleted almost to the point of extinction. "Newfoundlanders overfished for years," Mom had said once, disapprovingly, "and now they're surprised the cod are gone." And Dad, in a rare burst of anger, had replied, "What else could they do for money up there *but* fish?"

No cod. Probably no flatfish to spear, either, and no sculpins to catch with a line over the wharf. So much for half of Dad's summertime activities as a kid. Ben looked at the water and shivered. It was too cold to go swimming. Probably it would always be too cold, even close to shore where the water was shallower. Dad had lived here until he was grown up, right on the edge of the ocean for years and years, and he had never even learned to swim. "No point," he'd said with a shrug. "If you fell off a boat into the North Atlantic the cold would kill you before you had time to drown."

After a while Ben let his eyes drop carefully to the shore. Almost nobody was outside. He saw one man away down the shingle beach, doing something with a spade. There were some kids—boys on bikes—pedalling fast down the sea road with their backs to him. They were too far away for Ben to be sure if they were the ones from yesterday. A pair of little girls chased a cat into the garden just below him. Otherwise the village was empty.

But in the fall, he and Keith would have to board a school bus with dozens of strange kids and ride the long ten kilometres to school in Raleigh.

Keith's voice made him turn. His brother was running toward him, wearing his own jacket and carrying Ben's. "Dad said you had to," he said, holding out the jacket.

Ben shrugged and zipped himself into it. It did feel better. "In Ottawa the kids will be wearing shorts and tees," he told Keith. "The radios will be broadcasting sunburn warnings every day."

"You like everybody bugging you about skin cancer? Let's go down to the beach, Ben."

Ben hesitated. He liked beaches, and this one went on forever. Even if those other boys showed up, there was plenty of room for him to be by himself. Maybe there'd be tidepools or seashells. Maybe he'd find someplace to sail his model ships. He had made a schooner two years ago, and it had never even gone in the water.

They left the hilltop and skirted their house, Keith waving to their father who was looking out his office window. Then they followed the lane up past the Goudies' to where it joined a bigger road. Ben stopped for a moment, looking at Dad's map. This was the middle of the three roads that led to the

Branch. If they turned left, eventually they'd be out of Ship Cove and on their way to Raleigh. "This way," Keith said, pointing right.

"I'm just figuring out where everything is," Ben said, but Keith was already on his way.

The road meandered for a while. A woman came out of a white clapboard house carrying a basket of washing. She watched them curiously, pegging clothes to the line that stretched through the mist from her own scarlet roof to the bright blue siding of the house next door. Ben felt her eyes following them. He was glad when the road veered sharply downhill to meet the sea road.

There were several other houses on the way down to the sea road. The smallest was tiny, barely a cottage, and it looked older than the houses nearby. Its grey paint was peeling and the weathered roof sagged. As Ben and Keith passed it, a dog tied up near its front door began to bark. Teeth bared, it lunged at them, snarling, only to be brought up short by its own leash.

"Nice dog," Ben told it. The dog barked even harder.

Someone opened the front door of the house, letting out a blast of sound: squeals and shouts and grunts, then Tweetybird's cartoon voice saying something about a puddy-tat. The dog stopped barking, seeming to know when it was beaten.

A boy stood in the doorway. He was no taller than Ben, but somehow he looked bigger. Ben was pretty sure he was one of the boys who'd been up at the store yesterday. It was the way he stood more than anything, tough and self-confident, his ancient jeans ripped in all the right places, not like the ones the kids in Ottawa tore on purpose to make themselves look cool. This boy didn't have to worry about looking cool. He'd probably been born that way. Inside the house Sylvester Cat yowled. The dog barked again.

"Shut up, Yappy," the boy said.

"Good watchdog," Keith called cheerfully. "That his name? Yappy?"

The boy jerked his head, but said nothing.

"Suits him," Keith went on. "Dogs usually like us."

Ben hissed, "Come on, Keith."

Keith ignored him. "I'm Keith. This is my brother Ben."

"Stayin' up to old Jedsons' place," the boy said calmly, again with that jerk of his head. Keith nodded. Ben stared at the ground. "Easter basket house," the boy added with a faint grin. "Pink and purple, right?"

"That's the one," Keith said.

"Your dad writes books, we hears."

There was a hint of scorn in his voice. Ben looked up. "He won the Governor-General's Award for his last one," he said coldly.

"Good, is it? You read it?"

Ben bit his lip. He had tried to read one of Dad's books once, but parts of the first chapter had embarrassed him. "I read a lot of books," he said stonily.

The boy slouched back against the door frame. "Well, what *we* does—here in Ship Cove, see—is fish." His voice was so casual it was a mockery. "Or we hunts. *Outside* things, get me? We leaves books to the tourists."

"*I* like to fish," Keith put in quickly. "And we're not tourists. We live here."

"Takes more than livin' in a place."

"Let's *go*, Keith," Ben said through his teeth.

"We're going down to the beach," Keith said to the other boy. "Want to come with us?"

The boy pursed his lips, then grinned that faint grin of his. "Be down to the old graveyard in a while, if you're still 'round." He turned away.

"What's your name?" Keith called.

"Colbourne with a U," the boy tossed over his shoulder. "Ross Colbourne." The door shut behind him.

"I could *kill* you, Keith," Ben said furiously. "Sucking up to a jerk like him—"

"I didn't think he was so bad."

"'*We leaves books to the tourists*,'" Ben mimicked fiercely.

"Lots of older kids won't even play with someone my age."

"In a cemetery!"

"Dad said there was some playground stuff down near there. That's probably where Ross—"

"You'd make friends with a snake if you thought it'd play with you for five minutes."

Keith turned on him. "Well, so what? You never want to do anything, you never want to go anywhere, you just lie around and read or paint or listen to tapes. It's *boring*, being your brother. *Anybody'd* make a better friend than you. Ever since Mom—"

He saw Ben's face and broke off. Then he ran.

Ben shoved his hands in his pockets. There was string there, as usual; his pocketknife, a scrap of wood. He fingered the wood nervously. It was black ash. He'd been whittling it in odd moments in the car, ever since he'd found it a few days ago on the hike they'd taken in Gros Morne Park to break the long drive from the ferry. Black ash was a rare tree in Newfoundland, Dad had said. Ash, here, was worth something.

In the beginning Odin made an ash tree, the World Tree it was, whose name was Yggdrasill. He made it to grow out of the boundless oceans and hold the world in place. He made it to support the sky. In its highest branches he built Asgard, the dwelling place of the gods, and in whose highest seat Odin ruled. From Asgard the gods would make the journey to the land of men down

*the rainbow bridge Bifrost, and from there they would go to the
hall of the three Norns at one of Yggdrasill's roots. The gods held
their councils there with the Norns, for these three sisters knew
even more than Odin himself, yet they could not leave Yggdrasill
to come to Asgard. The protection of the World Tree was their con-
stant duty, because evil ones strove night and day to destroy it. So
will evil always strive against Yggdrasill, until Ragnarok, when
all else living will die.*

Keith was already at the sea road, looking one way, then the
other. Briefly Ben thought how small he looked, alone down
there at the crossroads. Smaller than nine, really.

Ben's fingers clenched around the scrap of ash in his pocket. He thought of how mad Dad would be if he let Keith go
off by himself the first time the boys were on their own in Ship
Cove. Then Keith turned left, hurrying off down the sea road
the same way the other boys had ridden when Ben had seen
them from the hilltop behind his house.

A twitch of a curtain in a yellow house just ahead of him
caught his eye. Someone was watching him. He turned away
and found himself looking again at Ross Colbourne's house.
There was someone else—a girl—standing in Ross's front window, staring at him. Yappy the dog lumbered to his feet,
watching him too, and growling. *Everyone* was watching him.

Let them. He had things to do. Boxes to unpack. Books to
read.

Keith would be all right. Dad had said you couldn't get lost
in Ship Cove. He turned around and marched back up the
hill, heading for the house that Ross Colbourne had said was
like an Easter basket.

Even an Easter basket was better than staying out here.

THREE

The ship was jammed already, and it was still being loaded. A boy was trying to tempt a pair of pigs up the gangplank to join the sheep already tethered in the open hold. His short cloak flapped in the cold sea wind. His trousers were pink and purple and did not go at all with his short blue tunic.

A lot of people were already in the ship. They had a pleasant look, flaxen hair blowing in the wind, voices raised excitedly to friends they would leave behind. It would be a long voyage. Ben could see that by the number of barrels on board. Fresh water, sour milk, oil, sacks of barley seed. Spindles and lamps, a porridge pot, crates and chests, skin bags to sleep in, hammocks, ropes, oars, a loom ...

But they were forgetting something, Ben noticed suddenly. Where were their swords? How could they defend themselves against the Skraelings without weapons? He opened his mouth to warn them, but his words came out muffled, as if he were far away, talking around a mouthful of cotton wool.

I *am* far away, he confided to himself. I'm not on a boat.

I'm inside, in my bed, dreaming.

"Inside things," Ross Colbourne scoffed. There was a dead seal at his feet.

That was what came of going someplace new.

"An Englishman at a rest-stop," the policeman explained wearily to the boy driving the pigs, "two other Canadians, a German on the highway—"

"I want to wake up," Ben said. No one heard.

The pigs were balking. A woman waved a ladle full of barley mash at them. Their snouts twitched, and they lumbered a bit farther up the gangplank. "Go on," Ben told them very reasonably. "It's still light enough. You want to read your book, don't you?"

They were sailing now. Waves slapped the wooden hull; the moon had set. What had happened to the pigs? Ben strained to catch a glimpse of them, but the night was thick, foggy, black as an asphalt parking lot, and wide, wide.

"Wake up, Ben! Come on, old son, wake up!"

He blinked, shuddering in pajamas sopping with icy sweat. The hall light was on. Dad was standing over his bed. One hand gripped his shoulder, the other stroked his forehead. "You were having another nightmare," he said gently to Ben.

Ben gulped for air. "I'm cold," he muttered.

"From the nightmare." Dad paused. Very carefully, he added, "Was it the parking lot again?"

Ben was silent.

"I hoped moving here would..." After a long moment his father took a deep breath. "Ben, I wish I could help."

"Only a dream," Ben murmured thickly.

"That's right," Dad said. "That's right, old man, it was only a dream."

◆

There was a miniature lighthouse on a rocky outcropping

down by the sea road. Ben discovered it looking for Keith, who had gone off again with Ross Colbourne and his buddies. Dad had sent Ben to bring him home for supper. "I don't know why you don't go with your brother," Dad had said. "We've been here four days now, and you hardly stir out of this house. And I'm sick and tired of Keith rolling in an hour late for supper every night."

"That's not my fault."

"If you were with him, you could make sure he got home on time. Go and get him, Ben, will you?"

"I don't even know where he is!"

"He didn't take his bike, so he's not gone far. He's always talking about that headland up by the new cemetery. That's where he'll be. Or one of the fish stages. Or the playground on the sea road."

"Some playground. Two rusty old swings and a pile of fishing nets!"

"Just get him, please. The fish and chips will be dry as cardboard."

And that's another thing, Ben thought, stumping down the sea road. Fish and chips every other day. Just because Dad's spending every minute planning out the new book…

That was when he saw the model lighthouse and the cluster of tiny outbuildings surrounding it. He stopped in his tracks.

He guessed the lighthouse would be about knee-high, but its position on top of the rocky outcropping put it above Ben's head. He supposed that was how he had passed right by it the two or three times he'd been down here before. It was a perfectly proportioned white pillar ascending to an eight-sided light chamber that seemed to be real glass, framed and roofed in red. Surrounding the light chamber was a tiny red wooden fence.

Ben went closer. There were windows in the base of the lighthouse, and an attached red-roofed, red-doored entrance—again, exactly the right size. Three other miniature buildings stood nearby, all complementing it with their white-and-red colour scheme. One was a lighthouse keeper's two-storey house, complete with framed glass windows, wood siding, attached shed and chimney.

Ben hauled himself up the first steep bit of the outcropping, then followed what seemed to be a path through moss and rose-root to the lighthouse. He crouched to examine it. There was a turning lens and a bulb in the light chamber, so it had to be electrified. Steer your ship toward its light blinking in the dark, and—

And bump right into this rock. Ben frowned.

But that was always the way with lighthouses. They were never erected to mark safe harbours, but as a warning to strangers. Don't come here, the flashing light would announce to newcomers. Stay away. Beware.

At the foot of the rainbow bridge Bifrost a fire is always alight to warn strangers off. There also is the Giallar Horn for the Watchman Heimdall to blow, if the strangers should ignore the fire. "Beware," the horn would trumpet through all the worlds. "Hear the Giallar Horn, and beware!"

The person who had built the lighthouse had been warning strangers off. But at least that person knew and loved wood and used it the way Ben had once done, to make small, perfect replicas of real things. Not everyone could see the point in that.

Ben wished he knew who had made it.

He was so engrossed he didn't notice that he wasn't alone until Keith's voice yelled, "Ben! Whatcha doin' up there?"

Ben got to his feet, looking down. Half a dozen other kids were with Keith, forming a semicircle around the base of the outcropping. Ross Colbourne was there, of course, and another boy the same age, a third who looked about a year younger, and a trio of girls. One of the girls looked familiar. Ben thought she might be the one who had stared out of Ross's living-room window at him the other day. His sister, probably. She had the same dark hair and eyes. Maybe she was eleven.

"Keith, my old son," Ross Colbourne drawled, looking square at Ben as he spoke, "seems your brother finally found something in Ship Cove worth his time."

Ben ignored the tone. "Does anybody know who made this lighthouse?" he demanded.

Ross turned casually to the boy beside him. "Whatcha say, Jimmie, do we know who made it, or do we forget?"

"Dunno, Ross." A wide grin.

"Dave?"

The third boy shrugged.

Ross shoved his hands in his pockets. "Seems as if we forgets," he said. He watched Ben's face with interest. "Matters, do it?"

Ben flushed. "No."

"Ben used to make models," Keith put in eagerly. "Ships, mostly. He won prizes—"

"Shut up, Keith," Ben muttered.

"Quit, did ya? Better things to do these days, I wouldn't doubt."

Ben began making his way down the outcropping. He wouldn't look at them. Loudly, to the ground, he said, "Keith, you're late for supper."

Ross said prissily, "You wants to scravel off now, then, Keith, or big brother'll wet himself."

Somehow Ben got himself down the last steep bit. He wouldn't speak to them. He wouldn't say one word.

A girl's voice called out, "The b'y who built the lighthouse is moved away." The dark-haired kid, Ross Colbourne's sister, nodded at him. "Last year," she added.

She raised her chin at her brother, who said disapprovingly, "You always got your tongue goin', Liss."

"What odds?" she replied defensively. "He likes the lighthouse. You likes it too. Went and helped that Brian build it, didn't you? Why won't you tell?"

"*You* helped build it?" Ben asked Ross. He knew his voice sounded insulting, but he couldn't help himself.

"Frig if I tells ya," Ross said pleasantly.

Ben had had enough of this. "Dad wants you home *right now*," he said to Keith, who was hovering uncertainly on the edge of the little mob. Ben didn't wait. Behind him, he heard Keith muttering apologetically.

He kept to a steady march up the hill road. Running footsteps followed, caught up to him. Ben stared straight ahead. "What's the *matter* with you?" Keith puffed. "Ben!"

"What's the matter with *me*?"

"You act like they're dirt."

"All I did was ask who made the lighthouse," Ben said through his teeth. "You saw how they answered me. Who's treating who like dirt, I'd like to know?"

"Melissa was okay to you, wasn't she? If you weren't always so stuck-up—well, they like *me* okay—"

"I suppose you think you're one of the gang," Ben sneered.

"I am. They don't even tease me any more 'cause I talk different than them."

"Different*ly*."

"Why don't you want to be friends with them?"

"I don't like them," Ben said. "Why would I bother with people I don't like?"

And for the rest of the way home, neither of them said a word.

◆

Ben lay on his bed surrounded by books, trying to ignore the sound of the TV in the front room. He was sick of it. Keith didn't seem to mind sitting there all day watching the same solitary channel, but after a couple of hours Ben had had enough. Dad was in his room. There was no one to talk to. Outside, the rain bucketed down.

Restlessly, he turned pages. The books on his bed were old favourites—two perfect picture books from his preschool days, a complete Brothers Grimm, a few collections of fantasy stories and myths, a dog-eared copy of "We Didn't Mean to Go to Sea." A couple of years ago he had only to open one of these books to be called away into the world it conjured up. But for a long time now he hadn't been able to read much fiction.

He flipped through a book of Norse myths, wishing he were a shape-changer like Loki the Trickster so that he could turn into something that no one like Ross Colbourne would dare make fun of. A shark, maybe. That would do it.

Or maybe he'd be better off being a bird, a raven like the ones that sat on the god Odin's shoulders. Then he could fly away, leave Ship Cove, speed across the earth and the sea faster and faster until he didn't have to think any more, didn't have to remember anything.

But even Odin's ravens could fly only as fast as thought, not faster. Thinking was one of the things you couldn't escape.

Like Ragnarok.

"Ragnarok is the final battle," Mom's voice said in Ben's mind, the lovely singsong voice she always used when she was retelling the sagas and the Viking myths. "It cannot be escaped. At Ragnarok the wolf Skoll will swallow the sun, and the stars will be quenched with blood. The earth will quake and the trees and rocks will tear apart. Bifrost, the Rainbow Bridge, will fall. Heimdall the Watchman will blow the Giallar

Horn to summon all the gods to the battle. They will ride against the enemies of Asgard, but Odin will be devoured by the Fenris Wolf, Thor will be poisoned by the Midgard Serpent, Frey will die at the hands of a fire giant. And then all will burn, all except Yggdrasill. Yggdrasill will not fall, but even it will tremble. When it is over and the world of man is destroyed and the high gods are all dead, only then, out of the dark, will life begin again."

"But how can it?" Ben would always say whenever she told the story. "If only Yggdrasill is left—"

"Of the world we know," Mom would answer, every time. "Nothing is impossible, Ben. Nothing is forever. That's the lesson of Ragnarok. Life always ends, and it always, always begins again."

"With no high gods? No Odin, no Thor? Who wants a world that's got nothing like a Thor in it?"

"Thor's sons will survive Ragnarok," Mom would reply, "and they will inherit his hammer. They will remember him. And the humans Lif and Lifthrasir will shelter from Ragnarok in the branches of Yggdrasill. They will have many children. Their descendants will mingle with the new high gods, and a new sun will shine brightly, and the new world will be filled with light and song."

"You keep saying *will*, as if it's all still going to happen."

"To the Vikings, it is," Mom would always reply.

"But the Vikings are gone. How can their end of the world be still to come when they're over with themselves?"

"Nothing is ever over with," she would say, "and nothing is forever." And there they would be again, back at the beginning of the whole discussion.

Like an unsolved mystery Ragnarok nagged at him, but there was no answer to it, nothing but the contradictions. Ben knew he had never understood what Mom was telling him.

He was afraid he never would.

He got to his feet, wandering aimlessly around the room, picking up things and putting them down again. He stood for a long moment in front of the shelves where his model ships were. None of them had been made from kits, not even the little sloop he'd copied from a magazine when he was barely eight. It was rough, and the mast was all wrong. But he still loved it as much as anything he'd ever done, even the Yankee two-master on the bottom shelf, which was far more intricate. Mom and he had finished that one just before Florida. He'd meant to take it with him to sail there, but there hadn't been enough room in the car.

Ben reached out a finger and stroked the Yankee's hull. Its silky perfection made him ache. Hours of sanding that had taken, he and Mom sitting side by side in companionable silence in the workshop, while upstairs Dad and Keith thudded around like elephants, clanging pots and slamming drawers and yelling good-naturedly at one another, making it clear to all of Ottawa that they were the ones getting dinner ready. With his eyes closed and his finger stroking the hull, it was easy for Ben to imagine that Mom was beside him again, her strong white hands tireless along the grain. Making it right, no matter how long it took.

Not everyone understood that need to get things right.

For the first time since the Yankee ship, Ben wanted to get out his tools and begin something new. He opened a pad of drawing paper and sketched a Viking ship with a square sail and thirty pairs of oars flying into a bay. But it wasn't right; the boat was a mere slash of lines. He ripped the page out and tried again, this time starting with the L'Anse aux Meadows shoreline the way it must have been when the Vikings came. But when he tried to draw the sod house settlement as a Viking sailor would see it from the sea, he found it was blocked by a gang of Skraelings lining the shore. All right, he told himself grimly, *draw* the Skraelings. Another new page. He tried to be Tor, sailing home and wondering what the Skraelings with their stone-tipped spears and arrows had done to the settlement while the Viking knarr had been away.

But he couldn't be Tor today. He couldn't draw, either. Because when he tried, there was only one Skraeling on the page. And it wasn't a Skraeling at all, it was Ross Colbourne.

Closing his sketchpad with a frustrated sound, he shoved his hands in his pockets and headed for the living room.

His father came out of his room at the same moment. Some kind of sports program was on TV, and the fans were roaring. "Keep it down, Keith," Dad said. "I'm trying to work."

"Sure," Keith said, and clicked the volume control without turning his eyes from the set.

Dad turned to Ben. "You upset about something?"

"There's nothing to do."

"Feel like reading? You're welcome to prowl through my shelves."

The double bed in Dad's office was the only sign that it was supposed to be a bedroom. The rest of the room was taken up with a computer desk, a table piled high with papers, and open shelving jammed with books and magazine files. "The novels are over there," Dad said, waving vaguely. The computer was on, the cursor blinking. Dad sat down and was instantly lost. Ben grinned a little enviously, then explored the books his father had indicated. Nothing.

"Don't you have anything on L'Anse aux Meadows, Dad?" he asked.

His father blinked at him. "Pardon?"

"Local history. Anything like that."

"All that stuff's there ..." He pointed to the pile on the floor beside his desk, but his eyes were back on the computer screen.

Ben ploughed through the stack. *Wildflowers of Newfoundland, John Cabot's Voyages, The Life and Times of Joey S.* Halfway down a title jumped out at him. *The Vinland Sagas.* For a moment his stomach felt funny. He hadn't ever read the sagas for himself, only listened as Mom retold them. He picked up the book.

"Find something?" Dad asked, lifting his eyes fleetingly from the screen.

"Mmm," Ben said.

"That's good. Have fun. I've just got to figure out this one thing..."

Gone again, Ben thought. He headed for his room, holding the paperback pressed to his chest like something very precious.

FOUR

The book was a direct translation of the actual sagas. It took a surprising amount of attention to read. Mom hadn't bothered with all the names when she told the stories, but here there were Thorbrands and Thorsteins and Thorvalds and Thorhalls, apparently several of each, to say nothing of individuals like Thorfinn and Thorgest and Thorgunna. A bare minimum of information was given about each person, so Ben kept having to flip back to remind himself who everyone was.

And then there was the style. It wasn't at all dramatic. More like a captain's log, a listing of events, one after another. Now and then people said things to each other, but never excitingly, the way Mom had told it. It should have been boring, but it wasn't. It was strangely calming not to have to think about how dangerous this trip across the icy North Atlantic must have been, or how these brave men must have felt, stepping onto the green grass of North America for the first time. The saga merely said that they went ashore and looked about them, that the weather was fine, that the dew on the grass tasted sweet. In the sagas, none of the Vikings seemed to think what they were doing was particularly romantic or unusual. The ordinariness of the account was enthralling.

Ben read until suppertime, then again until his father called lights out. In the dark he thought about Leif the Lucky, who had returned to Greenland from his first trip to Vinland only to have to take over the running of his father's farm. Knowing he would probably never make another Vinland voyage, Leif had freely given his brother Thorvald his own ship to make a journey there. But he had made it very clear that Thorvald could use the sod houses in the New World only on loan.

The gift of a ship, combined with the mere *loaning* of houses. The strangeness of this struck Ben forcibly. Vikings were nothing without their ships. Yet Leif the Lucky had given away his ship without a thought, when houses that he would never see again remained determinedly his.

Maybe he thought that by keeping his property in the New World he was laying claim to the land. Or maybe he wanted it remembered forever that he had been the first to live there. Or maybe, just maybe, Leif had really, really loved his settlement.

Leif had never seen a Skraeling, Ben remembered. Until Thorvald's later expedition, no Viking had ever seen another human being in North America. To Leif, Newfoundland must have seemed a perfect place to live.

Sleepily Ben listened to the patter of cleanly falling rain. He pictured raindrops beading the windows of the miniature lighthouse while it blinked its warning light steadily and reliably into the darkness. He imagined an iceberg riding the waves past that tiny winking light, a castle of fresh water frozen a thousand years ago or more, drifting and melting and changing shape and travelling on, a lonely magic amid the muted thunder of the waves. He wanted to paint it, that iceberg floating by in the silver, slanting rain. Tomorrow, he told himself, slipping into sleep. For the first time in a long while, he didn't dream of anything at all.

◆

"Here's your milk, my dear," the lady at the grocery store told Ben with a vague smile at the wall to his left.

Ben let his glance slide to the wall. A plastic cemetery wreath that said "Grandpa" hung there beside a string dripping with neon-orange fisherman's gloves. Higher up were some fishing rods and hooks, lower down a bag of BB shot, and in the middle a spindled case holding spools of thread. There was a shelf of patent medicines under all this, and another of cigarettes below that. But there wasn't anything on that wall to explain why the woman had smiled at it instead of at Ben. And she hadn't quite looked at him, either, not once the whole time he'd been here.

It wasn't the first time it had happened. Ben had noticed that a lot of grown-ups in Ship Cove either didn't quite look at him or stared with a kind of avid curiosity until they saw that he had noticed. Then they turned their eyes away altogether. They didn't look at Keith like that. Or Dad. Just him. As if he had two heads or something.

"And three loaves of white," the woman said, lining the bread up carefully beside the milk carton on the counter. She had a comfortable face, gently lined. She lifted her gaze at last, giving Ben a quick, anxious look. It was gone so quickly Ben almost couldn't be sure she saw him at all. When she spoke again it was to the cash register. "That it, then?"

Ben scanned the list Dad had given him. "Eggs," he said, "and butter."

"We only has marg, my dear. Your dad said he don't mind, last time he was in."

"Okay."

The door opened while the woman was at the fridge. It was Melissa Colbourne. Her dark hair was plastered to her head from the rain, making her eyes look huge. She had on a cheap jacket, soaked through, and she was carrying an armload of videos. "Hey, Sophie," she called cheerfully to the woman's back. "Said I'd get the videos back before one, didn't I?" She saw Ben watching her and smiled tentatively at him.

Ben's gaze dropped to the floor. He couldn't help it. It was as if he'd caught it from Sophie, not looking properly back when someone looked at him. But Melissa had smiled right at him like a normal person, and she was the only one of all the kids here who had been decent to him. He made himself lift his head to smile back at her, but she had already gone over to the shelf of videos and didn't see.

Sophie came back to the counter, the margarine balanced on a box of eggs. "Good job you brought back that lot," she said to Melissa's profile. "Rotten day like this, I'll have a big call on me videos." She jerked her head in Ben's general direction. "You two knows one another, I wouldn't doubt. Ben Elliott. Melissa Colbourne."

Melissa looked over her shoulder at Ben. "We met," she said, not smiling.

"Hi," Ben managed.

"Went to school with his dad, Liss," Sophie said, filling the uncomfortable moment. "His uncle, too."

Melissa grinned at her. "His uncle more than his dad, so *I* heard."

Sophie smiled too. "Long time ago, that were."

Ben cleared his throat, then went over to join Melissa at the video shelves. "That's a good movie," he said, pointing to one he'd seen back in Ottawa.

"Good for a laugh." Melissa eyed him appraisingly. Her

53

hair was drying in soft tendrils around her face. It made her look almost pretty.

"What was that about my uncle and Sophie?"

"They went together," Melissa said. "Everybody knows that."

I don't, Ben thought. "Does everybody here know everything about everybody?"

She shrugged, but at least she kept looking at him.

"Thanks for telling me about that guy—Brian—who made the lighthouse."

"No odds." Another shrug.

"Ross really helped him? He really did some of the building?"

"Some. He weren't any older than Keith at the time. You figure."

"So you weren't very old either." She didn't look very old now, Ben thought.

Something of what he was thinking must have shown in his voice, because Melissa lifted her chin at him and said, "I'm twelve, only a year younger than you is."

She knew his age. "What else has my brother told you about me?" Ben demanded. It was hot in here. He hadn't noticed it before. Really hot.

"Stuff comes out now and then. Like the way you're findin' out about *my* brother right now. He's thirteen, too." She looked at her fingernails.

"It's the lighthouse I'm interested in, not Ross," he said, hard and fast. *Stuff comes out.* What did she mean?

"Ross's the one to tell you about the lighthouse." She regarded him questioningly, then added, as if it didn't really matter, "Mostly Keith don't talk about you. He told us about your models, a bit. Ross were—" Now it was her turn to break off. "He likes them, too," she finished carefully.

Ben ran his fingers aimlessly over a video. A lot of people liked to look at models. But not very many people liked them enough to actually make them, especially not with the care that had gone into that lighthouse village. Months of effort were needed for that kind of woodworking. You had to be a carver yourself to know it.

"But Ross was really young when he helped with the lighthouse, you said." Probably he had never made a model all on his own. "He still make them?"

Melissa pursed her lips at him. "Ask him, why don't ya?" She picked out two more videos, apparently at random, and took them to the counter.

"You seen them two already, Liss," Sophie said.

"I seen them all, Soph. What else do you do, when it never stops rainin'?" She dropped her money on the counter, nodded at Ben and hurried out.

Sophie handed Ben a bag. "That'll be seven twenty-five," she said. And then, as if the pleasantry were forced from her, "How do you like livin' in Ship Cove?"

"Nice views," he said, handing over a ten.

"They is, that." She gave him another of her not-quite looks. "Your dad settlin' in with his writin', then?"

"Yes."

"People'll be comin' by, I wouldn't doubt."

"Sure." But there hadn't been many visitors. Mrs. Goudie had brought over the chowder that first day, and Dad's friend Ed Jefferson had dropped in a couple of times. But there hadn't been anybody else. "Dad's waiting for the milk," Ben said, scooping up his change and leaving before she could ask any other questions. As he pedalled off, the groceries dangling, he could see Melissa far ahead, almost at the highway by now, riding her bike as if in a race for the finish line.

•

"Our boat's coming," Dad said at breakfast the next day. "The old owner phoned while you two were fighting over the shower. He's bringing her over right now."

"Am I going to be allowed to drive it?" Keith asked.

"Of course you are," Dad said, straight-faced. "As long as you keep her tied up to the dock."

"Da-a-ad!"

"What's the boat like?" Ben asked, suddenly excited.

"Smaller than a fishing dory but a bit bigger than a standard flat—that's a rowboat. Nice and stable, shallow draft. The engine's almost new. By the way, she's just plain white with light-blue trim." He grinned at Ben. "Too bad, eh? Everybody seems to have been out of the pink and purple variety."

Ben grinned back. "What's her name?"

"What do you want to call her?"

"*Viking*."

"*Viking* it is."

The door opened and a man clumped in. "Mornin'," he said comfortably. He kicked his boots perfunctorily against the mat and walked over to the table, pulled out a chair and sat down.

Ben's heart thudded with surprise, and even Keith looked startled. But Dad smiled. "You must be Pat Burley," he said, as if it was perfectly normal for a stranger to walk into his kitchen without knocking and sit down at his table without being asked. "Want some coffee? It's fresh."

"Sounds fine." Pat Burley had a deep, weathered brown face and his hands were meaty and red. He loaded his coffee with sugar and milk and drank it down, then casually scraped back his chair and took the empty cup over to the sink and rinsed it, all without saying another word. Keith watched him in fascination, Ben in growing resentment. He didn't like the way this stranger was making himself at home.

"Got a lift back to Raleigh at ten," Pat Burley said then.

Dad looked at his watch. "We'd better get the paperwork done fast then. The cheque's not certified. I hope that's okay."

"There's money to cover it, I wouldn't doubt," Burley replied easily. While Lorne went to get his cheque book, he looked around with interest. "Makin' the place homey, I see."

"Have you been here before?" Keith asked.

"When Jedsons lived here. Always doin' somethin' to the place, buddy were."

"Doing and never finishing, seems to me," Lorne said as he handed over a cheque. "But we'll get things sorted out."

"She's a sturdy little place," Burley said judiciously. "Homey."

"You can do a lot with pictures," Lorne said. "We're putting up a few every night. The place looks better every day."

Ben surveyed the room. Now that all the boxes had been put away the kitchen looked bigger. The pictures on the walls toned down the green paint, and the plain wood furniture helped, too. The place did look better.

"Where's our boat now?" Keith asked.

"Down to Jefferson's fish stage. Buddy's rentin' you dock space, your dad say."

Ed Jefferson's dock was practically at the bottom of the hill. It'll be like having the boat in our own backyard, Ben thought eagerly.

"I was thinking of taking the boys across to the Viking site today if the weather stays good," Dad said, walking with Pat Burley to the door.

"Wind's from the south," Burley said, nodding. "What little there is of it. Couldn't ask better."

They left soon after breakfast, loading a backpack with

sandwiches, cans of Coke, a camera and Dad's notebook. At the last minute Ben shoved in his sketchpad and watercolours. It was a grey day, but the clouds were edged with silver. It hadn't rained since just after midnight.

"The guys don't know I'm not gonna be around," Keith said as they headed for the edge of the hill behind their house. "Can I go to Ross's house first, just to tell them?"

"Suit yourself," Dad said. "Ben and I will take the short cut." He smiled at Ben. "Come on, b'y. *Viking*'s a-waiting!"

The hill wasn't really very steep, but they angled their way down it to keep from slipping on the wet grass. Once, about halfway down, Dad skidded a pace or two on one booted foot, arms flailing, and Ben laughed, then laughed again as he found himself doing the same. Here and there among the dandelions and the rocks were gardens with potatoes and carrots growing sparsely. The nearest houses were some distance off. "Who owns the gardens?" Ben asked.

"Whoever takes the trouble to dig them," Dad said. "We don't waste good land here."

At the bottom of the hill was a rutted dirt track, all that was left of the sea road that farther east passed the grocery store and the miniature lighthouse village on its way to the headland. There were a few houses, each with gaily coloured oil drums outside. Some dilapidated sheds stood on pilings near the water. One of these was Ed Jefferson's, with its dock sticking out, a single boat tied up to it.

Ben scrambled up the rough staircase onto the dock, then squatted down beside the little boat, peering in. She was just as Dad had described her, sleek and well cared for, pale blue inside and white out. There was a pair of oars tucked under the two thwarts, and in the stern near the outboard an anchor rope was neatly coiled, with a strange-looking claw-like anchor attached.

"Like her?" Dad asked, smiling down at him.

"She's great!"

"Drop in, then," Dad said. "It's a good rule to keep your weight low in a boat, though I've a feeling our *Viking* isn't touchy about things like that."

By the time Keith arrived, panting, Ben had found the life jackets under the bow decking, as well as a second of those claw-like anchors. He'd also figured out the proper knot to tie up the boat, fitted the oars to the oarlocks, and was fiddling with the motor. "You're a natural," Dad said, watching from the dock. He added casually, "Of course, it's in your blood."

"Ben's not going to drive, is he?" Keith demanded, skidding to a halt beside Dad.

"Rowing practice first," Dad said.

"But Ben doesn't know how to row."

"He'll figure it out. Why not?"

Ben stared at him. Why not, indeed? "Get in, Keith," he ordered his brother as calmly as he could manage. "The middle," he added, "and keep your weight low, okay?"

◆

In the early days of the world, two wicked dwarfs named Fialar and Galar invited a giant called Gilling to visit them. "Come out in our boat with us," they suggested after a friendly night had passed. "We will catch fish for your breakfast."

"Then you must row carefully," said the giant, "for I cannot swim."

Fialar and Galar deliberately steered the boat into rough water by some overhanging rocks, and the boat was upset and Gilling was drowned.

"That was the beginning, Ben." Mom's voice filled his mind. "That was the beginning of the tale of how Odin found the Mead of Inspiration and brought sin into Asgard. That was the beginning of the long, long march toward Ragnarok."

Dad was saying something. Ben faced the shore and listened to his father's quiet instructions. "Pull right. Now both. Again." And then, "Rock coming up, your left. No, don't look. What are you going to do?"

Ben dug in with his left oar. He felt the boat turn to his right. "You're clear," Dad said.

Ben loved the feel of the oars in his hands. After the first uncertain moments when one oar would dig in deeper than the other, his body found the right pattern, and *Viking*'s zigzag path straightened out. "I was right," Dad said. "You are a natural."

Shortly after that, he told Ben to ship the oars. "We could row across the bay," he said. "But it's faster with the outboard. This time I'll steer."

Now that he was no longer rowing, Ben's arms trembled a little, and he realized how tired he was. He faced forward with relief while Dad started the engine, then opened the throttle. The sun began to shine.

"I'm heading due east," Dad said over the noise of the engine. "But you don't need a compass. The trick is to aim for Beak Point over there. See it, boys? Looks like an elephant's trunk from here. I'm aiming for that bulge in the trunk, about a third of the way down from the tip."

It's easy enough when you know, Ben thought.

"Southeast, now," Dad said after a while. "See if you can figure out how I've decided to turn exactly here and nowhere else."

The boat veered. Ben looked carefully around. Was *Viking* on a line with Beak Point and any other landmark? He stared southward. "There!" he shouted. "That little cove over there." He pointed.

His father grinned. "Quarterdeck Cove," he said. "That's where we're going ashore."

"I thought we were going to L'Anse aux Meadows."

"We can't moor right at the Viking settlement. Too shallow, and too many rocks."

Ben remembered the dying seal, the blood on the stones, and shivered. The wind was cool despite the sunshine.

"I'm taking us as close as a boat can get. It's safe enough, don't worry," he added, eyeing Ben closely. "I'm not going to shipwreck us."

There were, in the peaceful days of the Nine Worlds, two brothers shipwrecked. Agnar and Gerad, sons of a king, were rescued by the god Odin and his wife Frigga, and for many months they dwelled all four together. Odin taught the boys warfare, and Frigga made sure they learned the gentler ways of plants and animals. At last the boys were ready to return home, and Odin blessed them and told them to live worthily. But Gerad betrayed his brother Agnar, striking him senseless and leaving him to the scant mercy of the sea.

"Is that where we're going?" Keith asked, pointing at the little bay, peppered with rocks. "I thought you said it was safe."

"You just have to know where to go," Dad said comfortably.

The cove was enclosed by an alligator-shaped headland on their right and on their left by a high pyramid of sedimentary rock. "That's the way to the Viking houses," Dad said, pointing to the headland beyond the pyramid. He did something to the motor, and the boat slowed dramatically.

"Hey, Dad," Keith said a bit nervously, "I don't know if you noticed, but there isn't a dock here."

"Don't need one. We're going to moor under that high bit." He nodded at the rocky pyramid to their left, then cut the motor and put the oars in the oarlocks. "Get out those fenders, boys. Port side. That's your left, facing forward."

Ben and Keith hung the two bumpers. "Now for that second grapnel. Haul it out, Keith."

With some difficulty Keith got out the anchor, small and light and looking rather like four fishhooks tied together at the end of a long orange line. "Make sure the line isn't fouled," Dad said, dipping in the oars hardly at all, but somehow bringing the boat closer and closer to the rocky pyramid.

"What's he mean?" Keith mouthed to Ben.

"Coil the rope," Ben explained in a whisper. "Make sure there aren't any tangles." He wished his father had given him that order.

The boat was scarcely an arm's length away from the rocky pyramid that rose like a broken staircase to their left. "See those two rocks?" Dad asked. The rocks were right at the base of the pyramid—one in front of *Viking*, one behind—separated by about two boat-lengths of open water. "We moor between them." Dad picked up the stern grapnel anchor. "If I miss, Keith, don't let our bow bump. Fend us off with the oar, okay?"

Nervously Keith grabbed the oar and leaned out over the bow decking. Ben tried not to feel envious. He watched as his father threw the grapnel, on his very first try hooking it over the rock behind them. The boat bobbed, its forward movement stopped.

"Now for the bow anchor?" Ben asked.

"Same thing exactly," Dad said. "Why don't you take care of it, Ben?"

Finally! Ben thought. He took the grapnel, pushed past his brother, then leaned over the bow decking. He threw as hard as he could, and the sharp prongs of the grapnel went well beyond the rock. He hauled in tight, and there came the satisfying crunch of steel against stone.

"Good," Dad said. "Make fast."

Viking was moored fore and aft. "Fine work, you two," Dad said, smiling. "You'll be doing it all on your own before you know it. Now where's that backpack? I haven't been ashore here in years."

FIVE

The beach was heaped with shells. Fragile egg sacks littered
the tide line along with the gorgeously iridescent bodies
of thousands of small dead fish. "Capelin," Dad said. "When
I was a boy the capelin run was a big event. People would be
out for two days straight with dip nets and buckets, scooping
them up like mad." He crouched over a heap of the little fish,
and his face had the same thoughtful, distant look he had
when he was writing.

"Need some brains?" Ben asked Keith with a grin, and
tossed his brother a cauliflower-like piece of chalky white rock
that was astonishing for its lightness.

"Ycch," Keith said, dropped it and ran ahead to where the
beach gave way to grasses and rust-coloured mosses.

Ben waited for his father. In a while Lorne got up from his
capelin and made a leisurely path through seashells and beach-
pea to join him. "Always loved this place," he said.

The sun was still shining. Purple flags and yellow-headed
buttercups were bright against the beachstones. Back of the

beach were more flowers, rank grasses and mosses of every kind. Ben stepped onto what looked like a grey, lichen-covered rock in a boggy patch and found himself sinking into the rich black peat beneath. His father laughed. "Used to trick me, too. We called it rock moss. Don't know its real name."

There was an alive, clean, black-earth kind of smell to the bog. Ben breathed it in as deeply as he could. There was nothing at all man-made in that smell. The breeze whispered softly against the ocean gurgling at their backs. A gull called distantly. There wasn't a single other sound. No strangers laughing or shrieking or chasing each other or killing things for the sheer pleasure of it.

It was through murder that the Mead of Inspiration came about, and this was how it happened. After peace was made between the gods of Asgard and the gods of the Upper Air, every god of Asgard and every god of the Upper Air spat into a golden crock, and from the spittle Odin made a man named Kvasir. This man was filled with the knowledge of all the gods. He was as good as he was wise. He travelled freely among both the men of Midgard and the gods of Asgard. In Asgard he was valued for his goodness, but in Midgard for bringing peace among men and teaching them the arts and crafts that made their lives both happier and better.

Kvasir would go wherever he was needed; one had only to ask. And that was to prove his undoing, for when the wicked dwarfs Fialar and Galar asked him to come to advise them on a private matter, he did not know that the matter included his own death. As soon as he arrived they took him to their caves and murdered him and drew off his magic blood, which they mixed with honey and brewed into a mead that had the power to make anyone who drank of it a poet, a scholar and a seer. Fialar and Galar were afraid to drink much of the Mead of Inspiration, however, but only gloated over it in secret. And the knowledge of their own ill-

deed made them even more wickedly daring.

So it was that they drowned the giant Gilling. But Gilling's son Suttung guessed what they had done, and came for his revenge. And Suttung set the two wicked dwarfs on a rock in the sea to wait for the tide to kill them, and he took the Mead of Inspiration to his own huge castle on a mountain, where he stored it away in his treasure chamber with his daughter Gunnlod to guard it. And there it stayed until Odin came for it by trickery.

But trickery has its own payment, and the payment for the Mead of Inspiration will be Ragnarok, the end of the world.

Dad murmured, "I always feel bigger out here, somehow."

Keith rejoined them. "Let's be Vikings," he said eagerly.

"Viking treasure to whoever gets to that signpost first," Dad said at once.

The signposts were some distance up a gravel path leading to a rocky ridge. Keith was off like a shot. Ben chased him lazily. Funny to have signposts out in the middle of nowhere.

"I won," Keith said, panting.

There were two signs, hand-lettered and fading. One pointed east along the ocean and said, "Trail to sod huts." The other pointed south up the gravelled path, inland toward the ridge. "Parking lot and visitors' centre," Ben read aloud.

Dad arrived, using a piece of driftwood as a walking stick. "Viking treasure," he announced, and handed Keith a large Mars bar. Then he brandished his stick like a sword and growled, "Share the loot or die!"

Keith laughed. "Okay, but I get the biggest piece!"

"Which way are we going?" Ben asked.

Dad pointed inland. "I need to be out on the bog."

"What for? The book again?"

"I need to think."

"You don't need to be out on a bog to think," Keith said. "You've been thinking in the house ever since we moved to

Ship Cove!"

"So I have. And a lot of good it's done me. Not a single real page written, and no sign of any on the way. I need *room*. Someplace big and quiet. Elbow room for the mind."

Ben looked at his father in surprise. Dad had never talked about his writing when they lived in Ottawa. Everything was different these days. "Keith and I will try to keep quiet," he promised.

"Well, *you* might, Ben," Dad said with a grin at Keith's mutinous face. "But I wouldn't bring you out here and then expect you to stay by my side like quiet little mice. What I had in mind was taking you across the bog, showing you around a bit, and then turning you loose to go down to the visitors' centre or the sod huts or wherever you want for a few hours."

"By ourselves?" Keith asked excitedly.

"Why not?"

"I've heard of bogs where you can sink over your head," Ben said.

"Not this bog. You can get pretty muddy, but who cares about that?"

They made their way to the top of the ridge where they had an unobstructed view of the bog ahead: tiny pools and rolling rises and low, scrubby vegetation stretching as far as the eye could see. A weathered boardwalk snaked its way eastward toward a distant knoll that looked a bit higher than the one they were on.

Under the vivid blue sky the bog had only three colours— green, grey, and a dull, rusty orange. But once they were on the boardwalk, Ben realized that what had seemed like three colours was actually a miracle of variety. The green came from many different kinds of mosses, as well as pockets of juniper and willow and stunted birch. The grey was mostly the rock moss that had tricked Ben before, or the combination of white springy reindeer moss and black earth beneath it. And there was no actual orange, but only a blending of millions of tiny-bloomed flowers, yellow, pink and red.

Keith ran ahead. He wasn't interested in flowers. But Dad was walking slowly, breathing deeply, looking at everything, and somehow that made Ben want to, too. "Labrador tea," Dad said, bending over something that looked to Ben like white clover. "I haven't seen any for years." He pointed to another plant. "That's bake apple. The berries make a lovely pie. There are cranberries up here, too, and bunchberries and partridge-berry. We'll eat well in the fall."

The fall. School. That long bus ride with Ross Colbourne's gang twice a day, five days a week. Ben straightened up from the tangle of berry plants. "Where's Keith?" he asked.

"He'll be at Skin Pond by now," Dad replied easily. "It's just beyond that scrub over there. You'd call it a lake, back in Ottawa."

You, Ben thought. Not *we*. He began to walk faster and a little ahead of his father.

In front of them, the boardwalk came out of a brushy area and headed for a lake. Dad's long strides brought him level with Ben again. "Skin Pond," he said.

It was like an outstretched blue finger pointing ahead of them. On the right the flat, treeless shore was barely higher than the tranquil water. On the left the boardwalk skirted the eastern shore of the lake until it reached the base of a high, flat-topped knoll—the one they'd seen from Quarterdeck Cove. Here the boardwalk broke into two, one branch disappearing around the bottom of the knoll, the other taking a steep staircase to the summit.

They stopped at the edge of the water, and Lorne pointed to a wooden structure just visible on the knoll overlooking the lake. "That must be the viewing platform they talked about at the visitors' centre. It's new since I was last here. That dock at the bottom of the knoll is, too."

"Why does Skin Pond need a dock at all?" Ben asked. There were no boats moored at the dock, and none out on the lake.

"Don't know," Dad said. "You'd have to portage a boat just to get it up here. And the water's pretty shallow. I don't know why anybody would bother."

Ben was thinking of his Yankee two-master, the one he and Mom had made. He had never sailed her. And here was calm, shallow water. You couldn't ask for better.

Of course, a model had to have a proper harbour. Well, there was that dock. But you couldn't sail a model to and from the same place. He'd need a safe place to launch her. What were the prevailing winds in this place, anyway?

Ben caught himself up. A Yankee two-master tied up to a modern dock on an inland pond in Newfoundland. How inauthentic could you get?

"But I guess the Vikings thought it was worth bothering about," Dad said.

Ben blinked at him. "What? The Vikings brought their ship up to this lake?"

"More likely Black Duck Pond. It's just the other side of the knoll." He shaded his eyes, looking south over the lake. "I wonder where your brother is."

"How'd they get their boat up here?"

"That stream down by the settlement was bigger in those days. And Viking boats had really shallow drafts."

When he's born, I'll build your son a little boat, Tor told Gudrid. *"Not a knarr, for that would be too big for him, but in the shape of a knarr. It will have a sail, and only a few pairs of oars. We'll keep it up here on the lake. And then the boy can learn to row and sail in easy waters. Ulf will teach him about steering and winds. And I will teach him how to fish. He will learn well here. The first born to us in Vinland, he will surely learn well."*

"But there are Greenland lessons to learn, Tor," Gudrid replied without looking at him, "and there are Vinland lessons. Which must my son learn better, if we are to stay in this land?"

Tor didn't know how to answer his lady. He thought, maybe, she wasn't asking it of him, but of herself. He looked into her basket, half-filled with berries. Unas had brought a full basket back to Leifsbudir, saying that Gudrid had sent her back and that her lady would return when her own basket was as full. That was long ago. And so Tor had come for her, worried that the Skraelings might have hurt her. But she had been alone, sitting on a rock and staring over the water lapping the green shores of the lake, and the low bushes laden with berries beside her were untouched.

She was nearing her time, Tor knew. Women near to birthing were given to worry. His own mother had worried before his littlest brother Sigurd had been born. There had been nothing to fear, but no one had been able to help her, not even her husband or her other sons. There was nothing Tor could do to help the lady Gudrid now.

She shook her head suddenly, then looked up at Tor's anxious face. "A boat for my son, for his own," she said then, laying her hand comfortingly on Tor's sleeve. "That will be good, Tor. It will be very good."

A Viking ship, Ben thought.

He had never made a model of a Viking ship. He had tried that sketch the other day, but that was as close as he'd got. Funny. He had always loved the Vikings, and he had always loved making model ships. Why had he never made a Viking dragonship? Or maybe a knarr?

Knarrs were the cargo ships the Vikings had used to make their journeys to North America. They had oars as well as a sail, but they had neither the long, ferocious lines nor the terrifying carved figureheads of the warring dragonships. All the same, Ben thought, remembering the curves of the cutaway model knarr over in the visitors' centre, they were lovely. The Vikings hadn't been able to make an ugly ship.

"Dad! Ben! There's trout in this lake!"

A hand was waving at them out of a low patch of dwarf willow a short way up the eastern side of the lake. "Flat on his stomach," Dad said. "No wonder we didn't see him."

They hurried to join him, Ben dropping to his knees beside him. Keith turned a muddy, excited face his way. "I've seen two trout already, Ben. The second one's still there. Look. You can see right to the bottom. There's a stone. He's just behind it. I wish I'd brought my fishing rod."

"Maybe we can tickle it," Ben suggested. "You know, catch it with our bare hands?" He took off his jacket and rolled up his sleeves.

"Good luck," Dad said from the boardwalk. "They're a wily lot out here, our trout."

The water was cool on Ben's arm, but not unbearably cold the way the ocean was.

"It's great, isn't it, Ben?" Keith said. "Do you really think you can catch it?"

The sun glinted on the water. The trout was a shimmer of colours. It *was* great. Ben's hand hovered in the water, his fingers wiggling slowly and invitingly. "Worms," he whispered to Keith. But the trout stayed behind his rock.

"I think I'll leave you to it," Dad said suddenly. "You've seen the viewing platform. From there, put your backs to Skin Pond and you can't miss seeing the visitors' centre. The boardwalk goes straight there, or so they tell me. You can follow it to the centre and then head down to the Viking houses, or you can just stay up here and catch your fish, whatever you like."

Ben got to his feet. "Where will you be, Dad? So we won't bother you, I mean."

"Tramping. Making notes. Mostly around Black Duck Pond, I think. You won't bother me." He unslung the backpack and got out a packet of sandwiches and a can of Coke. "I'll put my grub in my pockets so you can have the backpack for collecting things. How does four o'clock suit you? That's just over three hours."

"Sure."

"The viewing platform, then," Dad said. "Four o'clock. It's some gorgeous out here, isn't it?" He smiled at them happily, and was gone.

◆

They didn't catch the trout. Keith ran out of patience long before the trout did. Ben was willing to give up too, because ever since Dad had gone he had been thinking about modelling a Viking knarr and sailing it up here at Skin Pond.

"Let's go look at that dock," he suggested to Keith. It wouldn't do for a Viking knarr's harbour, of course, but it would be a great place to see the whole lake.

"I want to climb the knoll first," Keith said.

Ben shrugged. He'd be able to see the lake pretty well from there, too. "Race you to the top of the stairs," he said.

Keith was off at once. Ben gave him a head start to let him win, and then pounded after him.

The top of the knoll was spongy with reindeer moss but solid enough to walk on. They ignored the path and went from one small golden tarn to another, eating their sandwiches on the way. The viewing platform was up near the far end, open on the side overlooking the lake. Ben climbed onto it. He couldn't see as much of the lake as he'd expected, but the land beyond it went forever, and looking the other way he could just see the roof of the visitors' centre. "That's where the other branch of the boardwalk goes, Keith," he said, pointing to the parking lot.

His brother peered out over the lake to the bog beyond, shading his eyes exaggeratedly. "Hey, Ben, what a great lookout! We could see the Skraelings coming anywhere from here, if we were Vikings."

"The Vikings did spend time up here," Ben said.

Keith nodded eagerly. "It'd be a great place for a house."

"There *was* something about a house by a lake," Ben said thoughtfully. He chewed the last bite of his sandwich, trying to remember.

Keith got tired of waiting and went off again. His voice floated up to Ben. "What a neat path! Hey, it goes down to the dock."

The path descended steeply past a thicket of spruce and juniper and stunted white birch. Keith was lying on his stomach at the end of the dock, staring dreamily into the water. Ben joined him, searching out the lakeshore for something that might do as a harbour for a model knarr. But the opposite side of the lake was depressingly uniform, and he couldn't see very much of this side because of the knoll jutting out. He'd have to walk right along the shoreline, if he was going to find what he wanted.

"Want your Coke?" Ben asked.

"Sure."

Ben held it out to him. "I'm going back along the shore for a little while," he said.

"Sure."

"You stay around here. The dock or the knoll. Promise?"

"Sure."

"And don't go in the water."

Keith's eyes were closing. It was warm in the sun. Ben made his way off the dock.

A harbour fit for a Viking knarr. There must be one up here somewhere.

SIX

Ben found his harbour on the east side of the lake, about halfway between the knoll and the place where he and Keith had tickled the trout. It was a tiny bay shaped like a half-moon. Extending into the water at one end of the bay was a narrow rocky point where he could catch a model boat sailing in a westerly wind from across the lake.

There was bound to be a good place over there to launch the model. It was meant to be: a Viking knarr sailing a Viking lake to this perfect little harbour. He would make it happen.

He looked across the lake, glittering in sunshine after so many days of cloud and cold and fog. Somewhere over there was the right place to launch his knarr. He returned to the boardwalk, then headed back toward Quarterdeck Cove. When the boardwalk left Skin Pond for the sea, he fought his way through scrubby underbrush and mud to the western edge of the lake.

A low, flat-topped boulder stood on the shore a little distance down from him. He slogged a path to it through trailing juniper, knowing even before he got there that it would be exactly what he needed. And it was. It was big enough to crouch on. The water here was just as deep as on the other side of the lake. Best of all, the rocky point of his harbour was almost straight across the lake from the boulder.

It was a by-the-book setup: launch point on one side, harbour on the other. All he needed was to make the boat. There was bound to be a westerly wind now and then to sail her in.

Skidbladnir is the best of all ships. It can sail over land and sea and air, no matter what way the wind is blowing. It can carry all the gods, yet when it is not needed, it can fold up small enough to be carried in a warrior's belt. The dwarf Dvalin made it as a gift for Frey, god of the winds. And he made for Odin the spear Gungnir that never fails to hit its mark. Finally, Dvalin spun hair of gold for Thor's wife, Sif, whose own golden hair Loki the Trickster had cut off while she slept. For the gods had banished two of Loki's children from the world and bound the third, and Thor had boasted of what they had done. And so Loki had taken his revenge on Thor by hurting Sif, she who had never harmed anyone.

Ben's hands sought his pocket knife. The scrap of ash was with it. He sat on the rock and began to whittle. But when he looked down at the wood, he saw that it wasn't a ship that he'd started to rough out, but something oddly threatening: an axe, or maybe a hammer. He held it up, frowning.

It was by Loki's persuasion that the dwarfen smith Dvalin made Skidbladnir for Frey, and Gungnir for Odin, and the replacement hair for Sif. They were such wonderful gifts that Loki wagered his head that no one could make any better. Another dwarf named Sindri took up the challenge and made the magical hammer Miolnir for Thor. Loki did everything a shapechanger could to prevent it, but in the end it was Miolnir that was chosen by the gods as the greatest gift ever offered them. Loki lost the bet, but he was too clever to lose his head. His lips were sewn shut instead.

The gods laughed at Loki when his lips were sewn. "Take a horn of mead with us, Loki!" they said. "Sing us a song! Boast to us as you always do about your triumphs!"

Loki did not like to be laughed at. He cut the thongs that had sewn shut his lips, but ever afterward he was scarred, and ever afterward he caused trouble for the gods. And in the end, when Ragnarok comes, it will be Loki's hatred of his fellow gods that will make it happen.

Ben looked at the little piece of ash in his hand. Ash for Yggdrasill, his mother would have said. He'd wasted it, carving a piece of junk. Well, it was too small to make a model knarr anyway. And after all these years he should know better than to start carving without a plan.

He shoved the piece of ash back into his pocket, then got to his feet. The huge cutaway models of Viking ships in the visitors' centre would help. He could make sketches of them and think through his own design afterward.

He looked across the lake to the dock but there was no sign of Keith. Ben churned as direct a route to the boardwalk as he could, then headed for the knoll. But Keith wasn't there, either. The low vegetation couldn't have hidden anything bigger than a rabbit.

Wouldn't you know it, Ben thought, annoyed. The brat promised to stay on the dock or on the knoll.

"Keith!" No answer. He debated going to the visitors' centre on his own and just leaving Keith by himself. But this was a bog. Dad said it wasn't dangerous, but all the same... "Keith!"

Ben went halfway down the path that led to the dock, but his brother wasn't there. "I'll give you my Coke," Ben bellowed. Still no answer. He turned and scrambled back up the path. Maybe Keith was playing on the side of the knoll. Its whole south side was a tangle of bushes, thick and secret.

What if some stranger had come around while Keith was all alone?

No witnesses. And a little kid all by himself.

Ben was panting when he got back to the viewing platform. "Keith!" he yelled, and there was panic in his voice. He heard it, and it was like hearing someone else's voice drifting through fog, high and thin and very afraid.

"Couldn't find me, huh?" Cheerfully loud, and very near.

Ben took a deep breath. He stopped panting. Even then, for a moment he couldn't speak. He had to make himself get angry before he could. "Where *are* you?"

"Right here. Can't you see me?"

To his left. That juniper thicket. Dwarf willow and a short spiky trunk of dead birch. A small dark triangle, barely noticeable beneath a drooping juniper branch.

Ben bent suddenly, grabbed at the juniper and held it to one side, peering into the dark triangle beneath.

It was a hole, and Keith was in it. "It's a Viking house, Ben," he said happily. "I found it first, but I'll let you use it, if you don't tell anybody else about it."

Ben took a deep breath, then let it out again. He struggled to find his anger, but it was gone. Keith had found a great hiding place and used it. That was all there was to it. He hadn't meant to scare Ben. He wouldn't have thought there could be anything to be scared of.

Little kids didn't.

Keith's face grew anxious. "It was you who told me about it, Ben. You said the Vikings built a house up here. So I looked for it. And here it is."

Ben looked into Keith's hole. It wasn't a Viking house, of course. It was just a level section of what was otherwise a steeply dropping hillside that the bushes had roofed over and walled off, making a kind of cave. The level area where Keith stood was mostly just beaten earth interrupted by a few roots and patches of moss. It was high enough for Keith to stand upright and still have to look up at him, and wide enough for half a dozen adults to sit comfortably together.

"It's a great hideout," Ben conceded.

"The Vikings thought so, too, I bet," Keith agreed, happy again. "I bet they never had to worry about Skraelings when they lived here."

"They can't have lived here, Keith. There isn't even a roof."

"It does too have a roof."

"Branches aren't much good in winter."

"Maybe the Vikings only needed it for the summer. Or maybe the earth roof fell in when it got old. The plants could have grown over it later."

That had happened with the original Viking houses, Ben knew. He looked down at his brother's eager face. It wouldn't do any harm to pretend. "Okay," he said. "It's a Viking house. Why not?"

"Come down into it, Ben. It's great!"

It did look great down in Keith's Viking house, very secret, very peaceful. Ben checked his watch. Still plenty of time to get down to the visitors' centre before Dad was due back. He duck-walked under the juniper, dropping it behind him, then half-slid, half-crawled down the steep black slope.

"Ouch," Keith said, scrambling out of his way.

It was darker than he had expected. For a moment Ben could almost not see at all. Then his eyes got used to the dim greenish light filtering down through the branches overhead. "Earth walls," Keith said, pointing to where the hillside jutted outward, forming one side as well as the front of the little chamber. "Just like Leif's house, right? We could build shelves here. Benches to sleep on, the way Leif's men did. We could put furs on them the way they did—"

"That sheepskin rug from my bedroom," Ben put in. "And I could make a candle holder."

"We could build a fire in the centre, like in the longhouse. We'd stay warm even in winter that way."

Ben shook his head regretfully. "No fires. Not with all these branches."

"Do you think we could sleep here some night? That'd be really cool."

Ben pictured it. A Viking house. The Viking harbour down below, his own Viking knarr peacefully moored in it. He and Keith catching trout and cooking them on an outdoor fire. Sailing the boat together. It would be easier with two—one to launch her and one to catch her. Maybe Keith would even help him make the boat. He had never shown an interest in woodworking, but then, he'd been awfully young the last time Ben had made a model.

It would be fun, the two of them working together. In Ottawa Ben would never have dreamed of doing things with his brother by choice, but here things were different. He imagined them sailing the model from one side of the lake to the other and then coming up here to the house when the wind blew cold or the fog settled in. Ben would read the sagas aloud. Or by then, maybe, he would have them memorized, and it would be just like the real thing, Viking storytellers passing the tales on to the young folk. And then Keith would fall asleep, and Ben would carve. It would be perfect. In this secret place they would be safe even if the Skraelings came.

So what if it was all just pretend? So were books. So were models. So were paintings, even. All the things he liked. None of them were real life, and who cared?

He liked this place. He liked it a lot. It was better than a Viking house. When he was inside it, no one would know that he was even there.

◆

It had clouded over again by four o'clock. Lorne was late meeting them at the viewing platform. "Sorry, sorry," he said, out of breath but looking pleased with himself. "Got a good idea when I was out there and completely lost track of time. But we'd better get moving. There's a storm coming."

They didn't show him their Viking house. They had pledged not to tell anyone about it, not even Dad.

The wind was up when they got to the cove, and this time there was no question about who would take charge of *Viking*. It was only a twenty-minute trip, but so bouncy they all felt a little bruised by the time they were back at Jefferson's dock. Ben headed for the hillside that led up to their house, but Dad stopped him. "Let's take the road. I need to stop at the store."

Ben usually avoided the store on the sea road because it was so near Ross Colbourne's house. But it was a lot closer to their own house than Sophie's store up by the highway. "We're out of ice cream," Keith said.

"Main course is what I'm interested in, b'y," Dad said.

There was someone up on the rock where the lighthouse village was. Ben couldn't be sure, but he thought it might be Ross.

In the store were three elderly women and a man at the cash counter. Everyone stopped talking when they came in. Dad nodded at the women. "Mrs. Jackson, Mrs. Lang," he said. He smiled at the third, who was little and stern-looking, with a tight kerchief tied around her chin. "Don't believe you've met my boys, Mrs. Grady," he said to her. "Ben, Keith, this is Mrs. Grady, my grade five teacher. I wouldn't be a writer today if it hadn't been for her grammar lessons."

She pursed her lips, but looked pleased. "Long way from knowing participles to writing books," she said.

"Long way," Dad agreed, "make no doubt." It was his Newfoundland voice again.

"Closed the old school, they did," Mrs. Grady said.

Lorne nodded.

One of the other women said, "Buddy don't write books much, here."

Lorne smiled. "No."

"Your brother doin' well? And young Ellie?" The other woman now.

"Fine, fine." Lorne turned to the man at the counter. "Hot dogs, Jack."

"Buns fresh today," the man replied cheerfully.

Ben had hoped Dad would take his usual long time chatting to people, but the whole encounter took less than five minutes. When they left the store the figure on the lighthouse rock was still kneeling there, his back to them.

"That's Ross," Keith said as they got nearer. "Hey, Ross! Whatcha doin'?"

Ross turned his head. "Light's not workin' right," he said shortly.

"So you're an electrician as well as a carpenter?" Dad said, smiling. "Keith told me you helped build this thing. Wonderful piece of work, b'y."

"Not so bad," Ross said uncomfortably.

"You look after her by yourself now, do you?"

"Brian, he wanted me to keep her goin', after he left." He wouldn't look at them.

"Lot of work in that, I suppose," Dad said, nodding. "You keep her painted, too?"

Ben hadn't thought of that. With all the rain and salt spray the lighthouse village was exposed to, the thing would probably have to be repainted twice a year. Hours of work that would take.

Ross shrugged.

"Ben and you ought to get yourselves together sometime." Casually. "He's good with wood and paint, too. He could help you."

Ben was looking too hard at the road surface to see anything else. But nobody could mistake the dismissal in the voice over his head. "Don't need any help," Ross said before adding, as if it hurt him, "thanks."

That night after Keith had gone to bed, Ben asked his father where he might be able to get some wood. "It's for a model," he said, keeping his eyes carefully on the television commercial that happened to be playing.

His father muted the TV. "A ship?"

"Yeah." The men on the commercial were not drinking the beer that was being advertised. They were pouring it and offering it to each other and throwing a football back and forth, but they weren't drinking. You'd think they would.

Dad had a smile in his voice. "Oh, Ben, I'm glad."

And the girls were all wearing bathing suits. The sun was shining. Everyone looked happy.

Dad said, "Will you need a lot of lumber?"

"Not that much." Eyes still on the silent TV. The ball game was coming back on now. Dad was missing it.

"Two-by-fours? Blocks?"

"Thinner than that, mostly." There was no point going into details. Dad didn't build things. Dad just wrote.

"You'll need hardware too, I suppose?"

"Probably." Of course he would need hardware. Mom would have known that without having to ask. Mom would have asked the right questions. Like what kind of ship he was going to make, and whether he'd made drawings, and how he was going to find out the historical details.

"You're not being much help," his father said after a minute.

Ben knew he wasn't. But he didn't want to talk about model-building with his father.

"I'm going into St. Anthony tomorrow to do some historical research at the newspaper," his father said. "There's a building-supply place near there, I think. We could stop at it on the way."

"You could drop me off while you do your research," Ben said.

Dad took a deep breath. "Sure." Then he added, "What about money?"

Ben hadn't thought of this. Mom had always bought him the supplies he needed for his models. "I ... don't know." He had about forty dollars saved up from his allowance. Would it be enough?

"I could let you have some," Dad said quietly.

Ben looked down at his lap. "I don't know."

"Look, Ben, I'm not much good with my hands." Dad's voice was even, every word measured. "Obviously I can't help you with your models the way your mother did. But I *can* let you have money, if it's not too much. Fifty dollars, say."

The way your mother did. Past tense. And so calm, so controlled. "Thanks," Ben said in a stifled voice. "I'll let you know if I need it."

"Frannie would be happy to know you were back at your models."

Ben got up from the sofa.

"I used to watch the two of you, you know. I'd stand there at the door of the workshop and watch your head and hers bent over the carpentry bench together and sometimes I used to think I couldn't tell which of you was which, you both looked so—"

"I'm going to bed."

"And you never saw me. That was all right. I never minded. You always showed me what you'd done in the end. And I loved Frannie's face when she was excited about your woodworking. I loved —"

"Good night." Starting for the door.

"Ben, please. I miss her. I want to talk about her now and then, not pretend that she never existed. She did exist. She—"

"I'm tired." Ben said it very calmly, very coolly. "I want to go to bed."

Dad made a movement to get up, then checked it. His voice was low and weary. "Okay, okay," he said. "Do what you have to. I'm sorry."

Do what you have to. It was like that sometimes. Loki was like that. Giant blood in his veins, but he wanted to be a god. And so he did what he had to.

"It was a great trick, what Loki did." Ben could hear the smile in Mom's voice. It was there in his mind right now, vivid and alive. "The goddess Iduna had been summoned from the earth by one who possessed the power of the Mead of Inspiration. It was Iduna's magical apples that kept the gods young. And Loki thought it all through, and then he arranged it so that a giant could steal Iduna. As soon as she disappeared from Asgard, the gods began to age. Loki waited until they were desperate, then used his shape-changing abilities to steal Iduna back from the giant. The gods never knew Loki had been responsible for her disappearance in the first place, and they were so pleased they made him one of them at last."

Loki had got what he wanted, Ben thought. But it hadn't worked out very well. Sometimes Loki got along with the other gods, but he was a newcomer, and there was that giant blood of his. Also, he was usually cleverer than they were. And so they let his lips be sewn shut and laughed at him and took away his children. In the end he hated them enough to want to hurt them in return.

It will be Loki's hatred that will unleash Ragnarok, when it finally comes. Yet it began most truly when Kvasir's blood became the Mead of Inspiration and Odin obtained the mead by deceit. Without this, Iduna would never have existed. Without Iduna, Loki would not have become a god, nor learned to hate. So all things are caused by one thing, and all, in the end, lead to Ragnarok.

"Ben," his father called, almost despairingly. "Son."

With his hand on his bedroom door, Ben stopped. He didn't turn.

"It wasn't your fault," Dad said. "What happened in the parking lot. It wasn't your fault."

Ben opened the door, and quietly, very quietly, shut himself inside.

SEVEN

Just after five the next morning, Ben was down on the beach to see the sun rise. It was huge and flaming and it hurt his eyes to look at it. Glittering light poured a red-gold path across the ocean. He watched it until his eyes prismed the light into a blur of colours. Bifrost, he thought, the Rainbow Bridge of the gods.

Aimlessly he wandered down the beach north of the miniature lighthouse. He passed the playground opposite the old cemetery that the sea had washed away, so that now there was nothing left but new crosses planted by the villagers for remembrance. This was one of the places Keith's gang hung out. Ben usually avoided it. But now there was nobody else around.

He had hardly slept the night before. When he had slept, he had dreamed. It was easier to be awake.

The sun was higher in the sky now, and no longer burned a path across the water. But still there seemed to be no one else awake. He might have been Lif, the only boy left in the world after Ragnarok. Lif had sheltered in Yggdrasill, and so he had survived.

"He *will* shelter in Yggdrasill," Mom's voice corrected him in his mind. "It hasn't happened yet, remember? And Lif will not be alone. The girl Lifthrasir will be with him."

Who wants them? Ben thought now. Who wants people who hide and keep themselves safe while everything else in the world that's worth anything comes to an end?

"It's not as though a palisade will keep the Skraelings out for long," Nils argued. *He let his axe fall and spat on his hands while Tor chopped doggedly on. "And our territory will become only what is inside the palisade. Theirs will be everything else."*

Tor had heard it all before. "Are you my cutting partner or am I to take these trees down all by myself?"

"It's not like the old days with the men off raiding and the women left alone to run the farms. Our women are never alone in Leifsbudir. Even on a hunting expedition we leave enough men to—"

"Your tongue is sharper than your axe, Nils Larsson."

Nils dipped the nearby ladle in a bucket of drinking water, and in one smooth motion doused Tor with it. "A hot day," he said. Then he stripped off his tunic and poured a second ladle over his own head. All around them the woods rang with the sound of axes chopping.

"Tell me the truth, young Tor," Nils said, when they had both blinked the water out of their eyes. "Do you really think building this palisade is honourable work for a Northman?"

"Karlsefni tells us what is honourable work," Tor said uncomfortably. "We are bound to serve him."

"Him?" Nils asked wryly. "Or his wife?"

"What do you mean?"

"It is Gudrid's counsel, this palisade. It must be. She fears for her unborn child. She will have a son, they say. How does she

know such things? Does she also know that the Skraelings will attack us?"

Tor frowned. "The lady Gudrid is not afraid of the Skraelings. The gods know she does not want to fight them, but it is not from cowardice. She…would deal differently with them than her lord, that is all. The palisade was no idea of hers."

"If she weren't here, we wouldn't be making it. Karlsefni wants to protect her. He wants even more to protect the son she will bear."

"To protect us all against the wild beasts of winter, Karlsefni told us. You heard him. There was nothing about Skraelings."

"Leif needed no palisade against wild beasts, when he wintered here."

Tor was silent. It was true.

"The Skraelings will think it a sign that we fear them," Nils went on. "By Odin's spear, it is what I would think, and I have been a warrior. Karlsefni is only a trader."

"He is our lord."

"He is no warrior. The Skraelings are. They would have attacked us already, except that we have shown we do not fear them. When men are outnumbered, they win by being brave, not by hiding themselves away like frightened children."

"We must build the palisade," Tor said, all the more stubbornly because he was afraid he agreed with Nils.

"Build it we must," Nils agreed grimly. "But when the time comes, we do not have to stay locked inside it."

Bowing his head, Ben kicked at the beach as he walked. One foot, then the other. Showers of stones flew ahead of him.

"Hey, Ben!"

His head jerked up.

"Over here!"

Beyond the beach to his left was the road, and just beyond that was Melissa Colbourne, kneeling in one of the tiny garden plots Dad had said belonged to anybody who wanted to work them. She had a smear of dirt down one cheek, and a trowel in her hand. "Got a rock here won't budge. Want to give me a hand?"

Ben hesitated. Then he climbed the slope to the road, crossed it and went to join her.

"You been out all night?" she asked, sitting back on her heels and regarding him curiously.

"No. Why?"

"You looks beat."

"Just up early. So are you."

She shrugged. "Same as every day. Dad says he'll have the skin off me if I makes a noise and wakes him, but I can't sleep past six. So I come here. Just me and the carrots and turnips."

"What do you do in the winter when you can't sleep?"

"Wishes it was summer." She gave a faint grin. "So'll you, make no doubt."

"Where's that rock you need help with?"

She jerked her head downward. Ben crouched beside her. He could see a bit of it, black as slate. She held out the trowel. "You get under her and pry, and I'll grab."

Ben probed with the trowel. The rock was a big one, one of those long slab-like things he'd seen so often on beaches here. He found the edge at last, and pried it up a short distance. Melissa's short, deft fingers went into the gap at once. "Careful," Ben warned. "I don't want to cut you if this thing slips."

"Got it," she said confidently. "Get the other side, will ya?"

He slid the trowel out. The stone settled into Melissa's palm. She grubbed the other hand under it, too. "Okay?" he asked.

"Sure."

He found the other edge and levered it up to where he

could grab it. It was as long as his arm. Though it was fairly thin, it weighed plenty. "Where to?"

"Beach. Some big, huh? Been fightin' her for two mornings now."

"Wouldn't Ross help you?"

"Didn't ask him." She pursed her lips. "It's my garden, see. It's what I do to help out, with the fishery closed and all. Ross, he delivers *The Northern Pen*. We each got our own thing, see?"

Ben nodded. They dropped the stone at the water's edge, rinsed their hands in seawater icy enough to take his breath away, and then stood awkwardly, not quite looking at each other. "What time is it?" Ben said.

"Seven, near enough."

"Dad'll be wondering where I am. We're going into St. Anthony this morning."

Melissa laughed.

"What?" Ben demanded.

"You says it funny," Melissa said. She deepened her voice and mimicked him. "Saint An-tho-ny."

"How do *you* say it?"

"Snantny's," she said.

"*Snantny's?*"

"It's our town," Melissa said. "Who knows better how to say it? Us or you?"

He turned abruptly. "Got to go."

"Thanks for helpin' with that rock."

"Sure," he said, and marched off.

Us or you. It said it all.

◆

"Hey, Ben," Keith said, "you gonna work on that model all day?"

"Mmm."

Ben didn't take his eyes from the piece of oak he was chiselling. It had cost him more than a week's allowance for the three pieces of one-by-one that would form the foundation for his model. Right now he was notching one end of the bow-piece to fit into the keel, the long beam that would make the bottom of the model. It was always tricky to cut wood diagonally across the grain. He remembered the first time he had done it, and the mess he'd made of it. Fortunately it had been only spruce. You could throw spruce away. But oak was expensive.

"You're losing the angle! No!" Tor's father grabbed his wrist, halting it in mid-blow. "You will ruin it! Watch, boy. Like this."

The master shipbuilder hammered the end of the chisel, hard enough to drive it deep into the wood, but almost casually, as if it weren't even slightly difficult. Not once in a dozen blows did he change the angle of the cut. A badly placed cut to the keel at the bow end would make it impossible to fit the keel to the bow-piece. There would be only two choices then: to find a new straight piece of oak for a keel-piece, or to cut off the mistake and scale down the ship.

Oak was a rare wood in Iceland. Tor's father had paid the traders half a monastery's worth of gold for this piece, so long, so straight. And now, after three long years as an apprentice, Tor would have ruined the keel-piece because he could not angle a chisel to make a simple notch.

The master shipbuilder gave one last whack to the end of the chisel. "Do you see?" He looked at Tor, and his voice grew less stern. "It is one of the most difficult jobs there is, chiselling across the grain into oak without losing the angle. You do well in most things, boy. Strength of the wrist will come with years."

"It's too nice out to waste the day working," Keith said.

Ben continued making carefully angled blows on the chisel. But Keith was still there, breathing heavily over him. "This isn't work," Ben replied. "It's fun."

It was another bright, blue day—two in a row now with no sign of rain. Ben had put up a card table in the backyard and was sitting beside it on a battered wooden desk chair. The sun was warm on his head.

Yesterday, after coming back from St. Anthony, he had spent a lot of time carving the smooth curve at the bottom of the keel-piece so that it would cut cleanly through the water and keep the ship from wallowing sideways when she sailed. The other two oak pieces were shorter, but they, too, needed shaping. The thin ends would make the highest points of the bow and stern. A notch would go into the thicker end of each to match the one at each end of the keel. When the three pieces were attached and braced, Ben would chisel off the sharp corners of the joins and make them the proper smooth arc.

"It's a perfect day for a bike ride," Keith said.

The master shipbuilder gave Tor the task of cutting the central ribs. Tor was stunned at this sign of his father's trust. After his near-disaster with the keel-piece, he had thought he might be assigned a menial task—perhaps the cradle that would support the ship while the building went on. But this! This was real shipbuilding. He stroked the pine block his father put in front of him, happy and doubtful at the same time.

"Pine likes your touch," his father explained calmly. "Oak will also, when you have a man's wrists instead of a boy's. When I gave you the keel-piece it was because you do so much else so well. Sometimes I forget that you are only ten."

"So, what about it?" Keith asked impatiently.

"This is a long job," Ben said, still keeping his eyes on his chisel. "And after this part there's the support cradle to make, and all the ribs to carve and attach."

"And then will the boat be done?"

Ben pulled the chisel back, shaking away a splinter that had broken off. The notch seemed deep enough. He tested it against the keel cut. It matched. Good.

He grinned at his brother. "You ever try to sail anything that looked like a fish skeleton?"

"Well, you don't have to make the whole boat in one day, do you?"

Six of the master shipbuilder's slaves were already at work under the guidance of Freeman Thiassi, cutting side-planks out of the straight poles that had once been pine trees. These planks had to be thin enough that they could be fitted to the curve of the ribs and tied there with tree roots. That was what made the ship flex with the waves instead of battering her way through them, and it was one of the many reasons why the Northman's ships were the best in the world. Tor would have been pleased enough to have been assigned to Thiassi. Instead he had been given the all-important central ribs, all on his own.

He leaned his chisel against the soft pine block. Pine and he understood each other. He took a nervous breath and raised his hammer for the first blow. The chisel sank in, the angle true.

"It's going to take a lot more than one day, Keith. I'm going to use strips of pine veneer instead of making my own side-planks, but even so ..."

Keith was shifting impatiently from one foot to the other. "Then why spend all day on it today?"

"Up in the bog you wanted us to be Vikings," Ben said. "We can't do that without having our own ship, can we?"

"We're not up in the bog now," Keith said. "There's lots of other things to do here. We don't have to be Vikings."

That's the trouble with Keith, Ben thought. He gets excited about new ideas, but it only lasts for about five minutes. "You could help me make the model," Ben suggested.

"What for?"

"For fun. And then the ship would belong to both of us."

"I've never carved anything."

"You could start on the support cradle. It's not hard. Viking boys younger than you did it when they were learning to be shipbuilders."

"Ross and the guys are going to ride their bikes into Raleigh. I said I'd go with them." He scuffed the toe of one runner in the dirt and mumbled, "You want to come?"

"Pardon?"

"You want to ride into Raleigh with us?"

Ben put down his chisel. "Yeah, right," he said sarcastically. "Drop something I like doing and ride my bike ten kilometres with a bunch of Neanderthals just to buy a candy bar at some other town's convenience store. Yeah, Keith, sure I'm going to do that."

"We're gonna explore Raleigh. Meet some other kids. You know."

Ben raised one eyebrow. "I'll bet Ross and the others don't know you're asking me."

"They do so. They told me to ask you."

Ben's eyes narrowed. "Now *that* is hard to believe."

"No, really, Ben. Ross said…"

"What?"

His brother sounded embarrassed. "Well, first he said … well, he said something about you never riding your bike."

"Uh-huh. And then?"

Keith muttered, "I don't like it when you keep acting so stuck up with the other kids. I wish…"

"What did Ross say? First the thing about the bike, and then—"

"It's an expensive bike."

"Ross said that?"

"Kind of. He…wondered what you kept it outside for."

"For show, obviously," Ben said sarcastically.

Keith mumbled, "That's what Ross—"

"Ross doesn't think I can ride it? Just because I don't show off all the time the way Apeman Colbourne does…"

Keith flared, "You were showing off the other day when you were rowing. Ross saw you. He said you could use a lesson. That's why…"

"How's anybody going to give me a rowing lesson on a bike?"

Keith said nothing. Ben's heart began to beat more quickly. "That's not what he meant, was it? A *rowing* lesson wasn't the kind of lesson he meant."

"You're so mean to them!" Keith burst out. "Yesterday when we got back from St. Anthony we drove right by Ross and Dave and you didn't even look at them."

"I looked at them," Ben said.

"Yeah, like they smell bad."

"You're trying to set me up, aren't you, Keith?"

Keith blinked. "I don't know what you—"

"Away out in the country with people who hate me, and my little brother arranging the whole thing—"

"No!" Keith said, shocked. "They're not trying to get you out there to…to hurt you. They're giving you one last chance to be friends!"

"What about all that stuff about teaching me a lesson?"

"They're gonna hate me if you keep on—"

"I get it now. They've stopped being nice to you, right? They've finally figured it out that you're just a little kid sucking up to the big boys!"

Keith went beet red. "I'm not sucking up! And they like me fine! They like me better than you do!"

"Get this straight, Keith," Ben said coldly and clearly. "I'm not going bike riding with you, not today, not tomorrow, not ever."

"Fine! See if I care!" Keith shouted. He aimed a kick at

Ben, barely missing the piece of oak Ben had just finished shaping.

Ben leaped to his feet and grabbed up the chisel. "You little—"

Keith skipped backward. There were tears of rage in his eyes. "They're right about you! You're just a snobby tight-ass." His voice shook. "You think everybody's your enemy. Well, you know what, Ben? After this they will be."

And Keith whirled and ran for the road, leaving Ben white-knuckled and trembling behind him.

EIGHT

Ben thought his father knew that he and Keith had had a major fight. But he didn't say anything. Almost a week had passed, with Ben working on his model and Keith off with the other kids and Dad writing all day. Everybody was being far too polite to each other when they did meet, but Dad was pretending everything was normal. At night he offered to play gin rummy with them, but Ben was always too busy with his model.

Sometimes Keith and Dad would play, and Ben would watch them while seeming to be doing something else. They held their cards the same way, Ben noticed, stacking their runs and pairs instead of fanning them. They both pulled new cards with their left hand and held the old ones in their right, exactly the opposite of what he would do. They both frowned at their cards before discarding. Their dark brows met when they frowned, and their sharp cheekbones got even sharper. Looking at them, no one could ever doubt they were father and son.

It had always been that way—Keith and Dad one pair, Ben and Mom another.

Every night before Keith's bedtime Dad would read aloud. He read in whatever room Ben was working on his model, unless Ben had shut himself away in his own room. But then Dad would just call "Reading time!" and pound on Ben's door until he came out to listen. The three of them would sit down together, Keith and Ben as far apart as possible, and Dad would hand them each a cup of hot chocolate and start the next section of *The Hobbit*.

Tonight they were at the part where Bilbo tricked Gollum out of his ring of power in that terrible darkness underneath the mountain. As Ben listened he couldn't help remembering how two days ago he had been caught in the dark up in the scrub forest back of the headland. It had been early, nowhere near sunset, and he'd figured he had at least an hour more for grubbing out tree roots thin enough to tie the model's side planks to its ribs. That was when the fog had come in. It had brought dank night with it, and Ben had found himself blind as the Viking god Hodur, with no one to help him.

He had got home at last, the orange fog lights of the village coming on just as he was about to panic. Hodur had not been so lucky.

The gods knew that blind Hodur had not—could not—have made the dart out of mistletoe, the one and only thing in all the Nine Worlds that had not pledged to keep the beloved god Balder safe. They knew that Hodur could not have seen to throw it at his brother. They knew he had loved his brother and would never willingly have harmed him. And yet it was innocent Hodur the gods chose to kill after Balder's death, not the one who'd aimed his hand.

None of the high gods could slay one of their own, on account of their oaths. And no man or giant or dwarf or dark elf could shed blood in Balder's palace, where Hodur grieved by day. It was only in darkness that Hodur left the palace and wandered in the deep forests, and then no one could see him.

But Odin, father of both Balder and Hodur, was determined that Balder be avenged. And so he fathered another son, a magical son by a human princess, and it was that son, Vali the Avenger, who came to Asgard with his bow and found Hodur in the darkness and shot him down.

When Keith was in bed, Dad turned on the ball game. Ben stayed at the kitchen table working on his model. He was attaching the side-planks. "Overlap them just a bit more, Ben." Mom's voice. "The same amount all the way along."

A commercial came on. Dad wandered into the kitchen. "Want some cocoa?" he asked.

Ben shook his head, his lips clenched around a couple of pins, his fingers busy tying a knot in the root that held the plank to the centre rib of the model. He had clamped the new plank to the one below it, the one he'd just finished with.

"Why is the wood dripping like that?" Dad asked.

Wet wood works. It had been one of Mom's most helpful tips.

Ben took the pins out of his mouth. They were short, flat-headed straight pins, but he called them rivets, because that was what the Vikings had used to hold each new plank tightly against the one below it. "If the planks are wet, they won't split when I have to bend them," he explained to his father. He undid the clamps and gently and carefully bent the plank so that it rested against the next set of ribs, then clamped it tight. While his dad watched, he pushed through his first rivet, then used the pliers to bend the sharp point flat against the other side.

"It's really coming along, Ben," Dad said admiringly. "You must be almost done."

"There's still the rigging, and the mast and sail," Ben said, licking his thumb, sore from pushing pins. "This is the last side-plank, though."

"Are you going to caulk between them?"

Ben nodded. "The Vikings used pine pitch and animal hair."

"Silicone would be a lot less messy." He saw Ben's face and sighed. "Too twentieth-century for you, right? Where are you going to get the animal hair?"

"I've got some from our hairbrushes, but I don't think it'll be enough. I'll have to use scraps of cloth, too."

Dad said, "Hey, what about using lanolin instead of pine pitch? The Vikings must have known about it. It keeps a sheep dry, so why not a ship?"

"That's a great idea," Ben said, pleased. He hadn't been looking forward to having to collect and heat enough pine pitch to do the job. "I could rub lanolin into my sail, too. It has to be wool, and you know how useless wool gets when it's wet."

"You're being so careful about all this, Ben. I didn't know, before, how much effort you and your—" He broke off, then went over to the fridge. "Sure you won't have anything?"

"No, thanks."

His father twisted the top off a bottle of beer and took several swallows. Then he came back to the table and picked up the piece of wood Ben had spent the morning carving. "This the rudder?"

"They called it a steering oar. Yes, that's it." Ben saw the way his father was running his thumb down the wood and added quickly, "It's still rough. I'll sand it the next time I can work outside." For two days now the fog had kept him indoors.

"I appreciate how tidy you're being," Dad said. He paused

for quite a long time. "It's been a while since we went out in *Viking*, hasn't it? Want to try her again as soon as the fog clears?"

"Could we go to L'Anse aux Meadows?" The model probably wouldn't be finished, but he could take over the sheepskin for the Viking house, at least, and some books and food and things. Keith probably wouldn't come, and that was fine with Ben. By now he would have forgotten all about the idea of sharing a Viking sod hut with his brother up on the knoll.

"Why not? I've got some more research to do. And it'd be fun to see if you can bring *Viking* into Quarterdeck Cove on your own."

"You mean anchor her, too? All by myself?"

In the living room the TV crowd suddenly roared, and Dad headed quickly for the door. "The first nice day we get," he promised over his shoulder. Pause. "Hey, all right! It's four to one for the Jays!"

◆

"Keith Elliott! You're not going out of this house until that room of yours is clean."

Dad was wound in a scruffy-looking threadbare towel, his hair sopping from the shower. He was furious. "Look at this towel. It was the only one left in the linen closet, Keith, and do you know why? Yes. You do know why. But I think the rest of this household has a right to know, too. Seven towels I counted in your room. Seven mouldy, stinky pieces of what used to be expensive terrycloth!"

With one foot already over the threshold of the outside door, Keith protested, "Dad, the guys are meeting early today. I promised—"

"Too bad. Your room comes first. And then inspection. And then, if I'm in a good mood, I'll *maybe* put you on bread and water for a week."

"It's the first nice weather we've had for days!"

"Is it? I haven't had time to notice. I was too busy looking for a decent towel."

Ben slathered peanut butter on his toast. Dad was really steaming.

"I'll clean my room tonight, I promise," Keith said.

"Now."

"Aw, come on, Dad."

"No, boyo, I mean it. It was your choice to wait till I'd reached the end of my rope. Now you pay."

"Doesn't Ben have to clean his, too?"

"You bet he does. The moment his room needs it as much as yours does. Now march!"

Keith flounced away, muttering.

The morning sun was streaming in the open window. A seagull was framed in it, white against the brilliant blue sky. Ben could hear the clear *peet-weet* of a sandpiper. "Coffee, Dad?" he asked his father, putting the kettle on.

"Ummm," Dad said. He blinked vacantly at the window. "It really is a nice day, isn't it?" Suddenly he banged his forehead with the palm of his hand. "L'Anse aux Meadows! I promised we'd go, and now I've got to play prison guard with Keith."

"Maybe he'll get his room done in the morning and we'll be able to go after that," Ben said. Dad quirked an eyebrow at him. Ben grinned. They both knew how unlikely that was.

"Sorry, Ben," Dad said. "With luck the weather'll be decent again tomorrow." He headed for his bedroom.

Ben didn't really mind. He hadn't been able to take his model outdoors for several days, and he had some messy jobs like sanding to catch up on. And there was still the rigging to work on. As well, he particularly wanted to start on the decorative scroll boards for the bow and stern posts. The intricate design he had modified from the saga book would be best carved in strong, natural light.

He had found a tube of lanolin in the convenience store up at the highway, and last night he'd finished caulking. He had put the model in the bathtub where it floated like a duck. Of course the conditions on Skin Pond would be rougher than in the bath, but the hull was seaworthy. Ben was sure of it.

His own design. His own measurements. Everything planned and made and fitted by his hand, no other.

And Mom not there to see.

He had used her chisels and knives and awls. He had used them before, of course, but this was different. This time there was no need to ask permission. They were his tools now.

That had been a hard idea to get used to. His tools. He could hardly look at them without seeing her hands gripping them.

He inspected his ship, trying to see it with Mom's eyes. Bits of it needed sanding. And there was caulk oozing out in one place. He would have to clean that off. He liked the pine veneer planking and the long, smooth sweep of the keel and gunwales. The bow and stern were pretty good. They would look even better when the scroll boards were attached. The steering-oar connection was one of the best things he'd ever done.

Mom would have liked the model.

"I had hoped," the master shipbuilder said, "that now that you are a man and have learned your craft so well you could stay with me. But business is slow, and there are Gardi and Eyjolf. They, too, are my sons, and older than you."

"They have not my skill with wood," Tor said bravely enough, though not looking at his father. Instead he stared into the hold of the ship Fairhorn, *his first vessel. He alone had had the making of her. He was sure that even his father could have done no better.*

"It is true you have the best hands of all my sons," the master ship-builder agreed. "But Gardi is quite good, and Eyjolf skillful enough. Besides, this Thorfinn Karlsefni has offered for you particularly."

"Why me?"

"He wanted someone young, someone without a wife. His trading journeys take months and years at a time. He lost his last shipbuilder on the voyage from Norway. He came to me to seek another, and saw your Fairhorn. He asked, and I have agreed. You will do well with him."

Months and years. Tor stared hard into Fairhorn's empty hold. "Where is he going from here?"

"Greenland first. After that, who knows? There is talk of a New World across the seas to the west. Perhaps you will go there."

Tor cleared his throat. "So I am to be ... Karlsefni's man?"

"That is no small thing. He is a wealthy trader and generous and just to his men. I would not have agreed to let you go if he were not."

"But I will be only one man among many."

"No fine shipbuilder is ever only that," his father said. "Karlsefni is nothing without his ship. He needs you to keep her seaworthy, and perhaps to add to his fleet. You will be Karlsefni's man as you have been mine, but there will be no other man he will value more. When you have joined his crew, you will understand."

"I might not see you again," Tor said. "Not my mother, or little Sigurd. I won't see Fairhorn again."

"It is always the way," his father said. "First the having, and then the letting go."

Ben carried the card table and chair out into the backyard. Then he got his sandpaper and pencil and the design for the scroll boards and his carving tools. Last of all he brought his model out into the sun.

A Viking was nothing without his ship.

◆

The morning sun climbed. Ben placed his card table away from the shadow of the house and turned his chair as the light changed. He was carving a pattern of connected rings on the scroll boards, with every third ring replaced by a cluster of leaves. In the house the vacuum cleaner whirred.

"Well, if it isn't big brother," said a voice.

Ben looked up. Ross Colbourne, Melissa, Dave and Jimmie were walking down the lane toward him.

"Hey, Ben," Melissa said casually. "Keith around?"

Ben made himself answer normally. "In the house."

"Supposed to meet us at nine, he were."

"Dad's making him clean his room. He'll be a while."

While he was speaking, Ross made his way over to the card table. "Decent chisel," he said approvingly. "Get her in St. Anthony's?"

"Snantny's" again. Ben gripped the chisel tightly. The model was on the other side of the table from him. He wanted to reach across and pull the little ship out of sight, but he wouldn't give Ross the satisfaction.

Ross peered at the model where it rested in the stand Ben had made for it. He squatted to examine it in profile. For a long moment he said nothing. Then he stood up again, shaking his head. "Keith said you was makin' a model to sail for real. He get it wrong, or what?" He picked up the model and turned it upside down. "Keel's your problem. Not deep enough, see?" He tapped the bottom with his fingertip. "She'll sail like a paper cup."

Ben gripped the edge of the table so hard his knuckles went white. "Put it down," he said as slowly and carefully as if the rage in him were something solid in his mouth, something big and choking that he had to form the words around.

"It's a dumb thing to be at, makin' a boat that'll side-slip soon's you puts her in the water."

Ben shoved back his chair. "Put...it...down."

Ross pursed his lips at him, then very casually put the model back on its stand. The other two boys hurried over. Melissa hovered uncertainly.

"She won't sail," Ross said calmly. "Guarantee you she won't."

"She will."

"Jimmie, will she sail?"

"No way, my son," one of the pimply-faced boys answered promptly. "Not enough keel."

"See?" Ross said patiently to Ben. "Jimmie's dad makes boats down to St. Anthony's. He knows."

"She's a Viking ship," Ben said. His voice was getting louder. "Viking ships had just a single timber for the keel. It's the way they made them."

"Vikings wouldn't be that stun," Jimmie said confidently.

"Look, I did my research—"

"Books, again," Ross said pityingly.

"I don't suppose you even *can* read," Ben replied, trying for an equally pitying note in his own voice. "I mean, this is Newfoundland, after all."

There was dead silence. Ben could hear his own heart thudding. That was wrong, he thought. I shouldn't have—

He glanced over at Melissa. She was staring at him, her face hard.

Suddenly two voices spoke at once.

"Now just a minute—"

"We goes to school, you—"

"He'll be goin' at the Newfie jokes next," Ross said with dangerous calm. "You wants a laugh, Davie, you better listen."

"Where do he get off, tellin' us we're too dumb to—?"

"Shut it, Jimmie."

"Look," Ben said, "I didn't mean—"

"Sure," Ross replied, full of contempt.

Okay, Ben thought. You don't want an apology. Fine. He raised his chin defiantly. "I'll bet you twenty bucks my ship will sail."

"She'll never sail," Ross said, softly and dangerously. "Guarantee you she won't." He turned to his friends. "Things to do, b'ys."

They swaggered off. Melissa didn't move till they were on the track ahead of her. She only stared at Ben, and there was an icy, set expression in her eyes. He couldn't match that expression when he looked back at her. He found, to his own surprise, he didn't feel right about looking at her at all. Then she shook her head, slowly and with a finality that left Ben feeling oddly sick, and followed the boys.

Ben watched them go. All right, so he'd implied Newfoundlanders were too dumb to read. It was a national joke, wasn't it, the dumb Newfie? But she should know he didn't mean it. He had tried to apologize. And after all, his own father was a Newfoundlander. Anyway, what right did those boys have to come over here and criticize his work? They had insulted him first...

She'll never sail. Had Ross meant it as threateningly as it had sounded? Ross wouldn't *do* anything to his model, would he? He made models himself. Surely he wouldn't—

Guarantee you she won't.

Hands suddenly trembling, Ben picked up his model and the scroll boards and took them inside. He would work better in the kitchen than on the rickety old card table. The sun wasn't that bright, anyway.

He'd already put in a full week's work on the little ship, and several days remained before she'd be finished. And she had cost him money.

Work, time, money...Ben shook his head bewilderedly.

That wasn't what mattered. What mattered was the ship herself. She was alive to him now. No, not quite yet. She wouldn't be alive until he set her free on Skin Pond. He could see her in his mind's eye, scudding across the water, the wind filling her sail, his Viking ship under sail, leaving this place and its Skraelings behind forever and ever.

It didn't make sense, and he knew it. Skin Pond was landlocked. But that was what his model was to him. She was a Viking ship, and when you had a Viking ship you could go anywhere. She wasn't done yet. But when she was, she wouldn't be just an ordinary little model. She would be alive. Alive, not dead and gone like the Vikings, or any of the other things Ben cared about.

He would protect her. Whatever happened, whatever he had to do, he would protect her.

NINE

"I think it's time we started dropping in on our neighbours," Dad said at breakfast the next morning.

"Ross's house?" Keith asked at once.

"For today I was thinking of the Goudies."

Ben had seen Mrs. Goudie quite a few times since the day she'd brought over the chowder, but mostly at a distance, coming and going to her part-time job in St. Anthony. She was pretty and pregnant and she never failed to wave when she saw them. Mr. Goudie had been in the fishery, but now he was busy building some kind of addition to the far side of his house. Ben had never seen him close up.

Keith said, "I had to clean my room yesterday. It's not fair to waste two good days in a row."

For once Ben agreed with him. "You promised we'd go out in *Viking*," he said.

"The wind today isn't safe for Quarterdeck Cove. Anyway, I do think it's time we visited our neighbours."

"What are we going to do, walk into their kitchen the way

that guy did, the guy who sold us *Viking*?"

"It's what people do in the outports, when they think you belong," Dad said.

"Nobody besides him thinks we do, then."

Dad said easily, "Ed drops in. And Sophie from the store came by that night you were late getting back in the fog. Can't blame the others for making sure we're really going to stay before they start going out of their way to be friends."

"The kids are friends with me," Keith put in.

Dad nodded. "But I'm different. I'm a Ship Cove b'y, and I left. Nothing so odd about that. Lots of kids have to leave the outports to find work. But after twenty years away I came back to live, and that is odd. Also, I'm a writer—not exactly the kind of occupation people have in the outports. And, well, there'll be other rumours, too."

"Like what?"

"Oh, there are always rumours in an outport."

"Haven't you got any *friends* left here?" Ben asked, not quite able to keep the hostility out of his voice. What about that first day at L'Anse aux Meadows when Dad had talked about all the connections he had?

"Ed, of course. And Sophie—though she was always more Dave's friend than mine. The thing is, most of my friends left Ship Cove pretty soon after I did. And their parents haven't seen me since I was a cocky kid who was always making it clear I was destined for better things than they could offer."

"*You* were cocky?" Keith asked curiously.

"Is that so hard to believe?"

"Yes."

Dad smiled a little. "Well, I suppose twenty years can iron the cockiness out of the worst of us. Ottawa can take some of the credit, too. It's hard to keep on blowing your own horn in a town where everybody else is doing the same thing."

"The people I knew in Ottawa weren't like that," Ben put in.

"Maybe not."

"And you had lots of friends there. They used to invite us over."

"Yes, Ben, we had friends. But we lived twenty years in one neighbourhood in Ottawa, and we never even knew our next-door neighbours' first names. It's different in the outports. There'll be feuds and gossip and disagreements forever, but basically, once you're accepted, you're part of everything and everything's part of you. Which is why I think it's time we started visiting. Because in a place like Ship Cove, if your neighbours aren't your friends, nobody will be."

Ben looked down at the table. It wasn't his fault that the only neighbours near his age were people like Ross and Dave and Jimmy and Melissa. It wasn't his fault that they hated him.

Dad was going on. "So let's get Mrs. Goudie some chocolates or something in return for her chowder, and then we'll go over, okay?"

"I've got fishing to do," Keith whined. "The guys changed it to today because of me having to clean my room. I'm supposed to meet them in ten minutes."

"Keith, you should check with me before you make plans."

"*You* should check with *me*!" Keith muttered, just loud enough.

Dad frowned at him. "That's smelling distance of nasty, boyo. But there's some truth to it, I suppose. Okay, you're off the hook. At least your brother knows how to be polite." He turned pointedly away from Keith and pulled out a ten-dollar bill. "Will you ride over to Sophie's and get something for Mrs. Goudie, Ben?" Ben nodded quickly, took the money and left.

There were three bikes in front of the store. Two of them

were much too small for any of Ross's gang, and so Ben wasn't worried. When he went in, though, the first person he saw was Melissa, leaning against the video display, watching a couple of little girls fingering chocolate bars at the candy counter.

He took a deep breath and went over to her. "Hi, Melissa."

She examined her fingernails. "You're funny, aren't you?"

"What do you mean?"

"Sayin' hi to a dumb Newfie."

"I don't think you're dumb."

"Don't you?" Melissa said distantly. She called to the little girls at the candy counter. "Sally! Jess! Come on now. You goin' to make your minds up?"

The littler one came over. She had long blonde curls and solemn eyes. "Caramilk," she said. "And bubblegum, and another Caramilk." She turned to Ben. "I seen you before. Up to the hill."

"They lives on the sea road," Melissa explained to Ben, though still as if he were a long way from her. "Under your house, more or less."

"I remember you," Ben said to the girl. "You've got a cat, don't you?"

"Big 'un," the little girl said, nodding. She dimpled. "He don't like wearin' dresses, but Sally and me, we—"

"Jess," Melissa said. "Go get Sally before she eats what she can't pay for."

The little girl marched importantly off. "You babysitting them?" Ben asked.

Melissa shrugged.

"How's your garden doing?"

She shrugged again.

"Okay," Ben said. "I'm sorry about yesterday. Ross made me mad. That was all. I just got mad." He looked at the floor. "I wasn't mad at you."

"You don't get it, do you?" She looked at him squarely. "We sticks together, here."

"So if Ross is mad at me, you are?" He frowned. "That's the way it works?"

"It *haven't* worked like that. I tried, didn't I? But you don't want to try back. I mean, we all knows you had a hard time before you got here, but that don't mean—"

"What's Keith been telling you?" Noise zigzagged through his skull, something he had heard a long time ago, surfacing again. Scared, he pressed his fingers into his temples. "What did Keith say?"

She stared at him. "Nothin' everybody didn't already know."

He stopped rubbing his head and grabbed her by the elbow, shaking it hard. "What did my damn brother tell you?"

"Let go my arm," Melissa said.

"Not till you tell me what Keith said."

"Let go!"

Sophie left her counter and came over. "Need some help, my dear?" she asked Melissa, but she was looking fixedly at Ben's hand on Melissa's elbow.

Ben blinked stupidly at Sophie. All at once, very fast, he dropped Melissa's arm. He stood there, concentrating hard on not shaking.

"I already went and picked out the video, Soph," Melissa said casually. "We're gettin' *The Little Mermaid* and about ten Caramilks, looks like."

She tossed the video from one hand to the other, smiled firmly at Sophie, and went over to the candy counter where both girls were unwrapping chocolate bars.

For once Sophie was looking at Ben, really looking at him. She seemed not to know whether to be angry with him or sad. "What can I get you?" she asked, as if it were hard for her to speak normally.

Ben lifted his chin. He would not shake. He would *not*. The noise was back in his head, a rising and falling wail interrupted by uneven drumming. "Have you got any chocolates?"

Silently she turned and led the way to a counter. Ben took the first box he saw, then headed for the cash register. The two little girls flattened themselves against the candy counter when they saw him coming, and Melissa made a big deal about wiping their faces. "Will that be all?" Sophie asked formally.

Ben managed a nod. His heart was pounding. He wanted to get out of here. Out of this store, out of Ship Cove. Out!

His bike had fallen while he'd been in the store. He jerked it upright, then threw himself on it. The chocolates banged against his knee as he pedalled. Serve Dad right if they were all crushed. Let him get his own presents the next time.

There were always rumours in an outport. Dad had said it. Dad had known the way people would talk about them, the way they'd find things out. And what they couldn't find out on their own, Keith would tell them.

Had already told them.

Don't think about it. Don't.

It was during Thor's mission to fetch a brewing kettle from the giant Hymir that he went fishing for his breakfast. He rowed far and far, Hymir with him. Land grew distant, and still Thor rowed. Finally Hymir said uneasily, "Now we must turn back, for here we are above the ocean depths where rests the Midgard Serpent."

Thor laughed. "I shall see the face of that serpent." He made ready a very stout line and a bull's head for bait. Then he lowered it to the bottom of the sea.

Hymir pulled up whales two at a time and flung them into the boat. "That will be enough," he said. "Even you cannot eat more than this."

"Wait," Thor said. "Wait."

Suddenly his fists crashed against the side of the boat. He shouted and braced his feet. The whole sea heaved; a mighty whirlpool opened around the line. And then, slowly, the head of the serpent came into sight above the water.

"NO!" Hymir screamed.

Ben was at the Branch now. If he turned left he would be out of Ship Cove. He could ride to Raleigh and beyond, ride and ride and just keep going until he was somewhere that nobody would know him and nobody would want to talk about him.

"Well, yes, it was his fault, you see? That car horn. *That* was bad."

"And if he hadn't insisted on staying out there in the first place, if he'd only gone with her..."

"Indeed I did not think to take an oath from the mistletoe," said Frigga. "I took it from everything else that lives or grows or moves upon the earth. But mistletoe is so weak and soft and young, it surely cannot harm Balder."

"Indeed," said Loki, then sped to the lonely oak west of Valhalla. There he cut a sprig of mistletoe, and trimmed and shaped it into a dart. He muttered a rune of evil over it, and it grew iron-hard. Then Loki put the dart into the hand of blind Hodur and guided that hand, and with it Hodur killed the one he loved best in all the world.

Now Ben understood. People not looking at him—or looking too hard. They knew. Melissa, Sophie, Dad's old grade five teacher, Mrs. Goudie. All of them knew. All of them, even Ross.

Feet drumming. A siren wail. It was in his head. It wouldn't go away.

If he turned his bike to the left, if he rode far enough, he would reach the sea. That was the trouble with being on an island and not having a boat. He would have to turn south then. There was only one road, and it went hundreds of kilometres before it reached a place big enough to be called a city. Even then, people wouldn't be like in Ottawa, so busy trying to make sense of new events they forgot all about the ones that had happened a few years ago.

He could go farther south. But sooner or later, he would always just get to the sea.

A Viking was nothing without his ship.

And there was his model.

He jerked the handlebars of his bike to the right. When he got to the house he slammed the box of chocolates on the table and was in the bathroom with the door locked by the time his father came out of his office.

"Just right, Ben," Dad called. "Thanks."

Ben didn't answer. He was still in the bathroom half an hour later when Dad announced that it was time to leave for the Goudies'. "I've got a stomach ache," he lied coldly. "I can't come."

"Are you going to throw up?"

"No."

"Can I—?"

"I'm old enough to be in the bathroom by myself!" Ben snapped.

Silence. "You don't want me to hang around then?"

Ben wanted to scream at him. It was Dad who had brought him to this horrible place, Dad who would make him stay here.

"If you're sure..." Dad said hesitantly. "I won't be gone long. And it's just next door, if you need—"

"Go," Ben said tightly. "I'll be all right. Just go."

"The number's by the phone," Dad said very quietly.

Ben waited. He heard the outside door close. He waited some more. Finally, when he was sure he was alone, he came out.

He went straight to his model. It was under his bed. He knelt to pull it out. Still on his knees, he ran one hand over it, then the other. He settled lower on the floor, the model cradled in his lap. His body bowed forward until his forehead rested on the bed.

For a long time he didn't move. There wasn't anything to be done. He was here, Florida had happened, there wasn't anything to be done.

The model was poking his ribs. Had he hurt it, leaning on it? He straightened, lifted the model to eye level, stroked it. It was all right. But there were the scroll boards to finish. And the mast to make.

He went to find his tools.

◆

Ben was lying fully clothed on his bed reading *The Vinland Sagas*. Keith had gone whining to bed more than two hours ago. Ben had ignored him, as he had ignored him for the whole of the last three days. Keith had betrayed him to a village full of strangers. He was his enemy. And the only way to live with an enemy while maintaining your dignity was to seem to ignore him and guard your back.

Dad had said he was going to take a walk, though it was another foggy night. Probably he was over at the Goudies' again. He liked them, he said.

With his bedroom door and window shut, Ben could hear nothing real, nothing but his own breathing. But the noise in his head was still there, a rising and falling sound he would not identify. It was loudest at night, lying in bed with the lights out. He told stories to the empty room to stop himself hearing it, stories about Tor and Gudrid and Karlsefni and the Skraelings, stories about the gods. Sometimes he fell asleep in the middle of a word. Sometimes he thought he never fell asleep at all.

He had worked on his model for most of the last three days, finishing the scroll boards and the mast and attaching the tackle and the rigging. It had been intricate, tiring work but now, at last, the mast was erect in its fish-shaped block in the bottomboards of the model, and the little ship needed only her sail and yardarm to be complete. He had oiled her butter-smooth pine planking to a golden sheen and put her to dry in the support cradle on the bedside table beside him. Now and then he lifted his eyes from the book and looked at her.

All day he had thought about what to name her. The Vikings had preferred strong names like *Hammer of the Seas* or *Surf Cleaver*, or names like *Fairhorn* that made them think of the gods. Ben had originally intended something like this for his model, but now he wasn't sure. The little ship was seaworthy and strong. She was clearly Viking in design. But somehow, to him, she had an air of delicate fragility that simply didn't suit the kind of name the Vikings favoured. He had kept a pad of paper and a pen beside him while he worked on the rigging, adding new names to the list as they occurred to him. *Wanderer, Explorer, Leif Eiriksson's Luck, Bjarni's Voyager* …none of them felt exactly right. Hoping for inspiration, he had turned to *The Vinland Sagas*.

They steered a westerly course…a place where a river flowed out of a lake…brought their ship up the river into the lake, where they anchored it…

Ben smiled, looked at his model and thought of its future anchorage in Skin Pond.

…built houses…Tyrkir found grapes…Leif named the country Vinland.

Ben yawned. Nothing here. It was getting late, but he flipped ahead a few pages to the next Viking's visit to Vinland. That was Leif's brother Thorvald, and he had come in Leif's ship and stayed with his men in Leifsbudir for the first winter. After that he had taken his ship and gone exploring in other parts of Vinland. Ben yawned again, and his eyes closed.

He was on a promontory between two fjords. His ship was moored so close to land that a gangway was all he and his crew had needed to go ashore. Trees lined the sandy beach, green and black in the brilliant dawn. The water glittered. A salmon leaped in a shower of silver. There was warmth in the breeze, the smell of flowers. He thought he had never seen a place so beautiful.

"We should settle here," he told his men. "Bring our women and children and build homes that will put Leifsbudir to shame. This is the place for it, beyond a doubt."

"We do not know that, Lord Thorvald," his man Ketil objected. "There may be wild beasts, or evil dwarfs or giants. We are far from Greenland."

Thorvald laughed. "This is Vinland, not Jotunheim. There is no Fenris Wolf or Midgard Serpent here."

He walked a distance, calculating where to build his settlement. He bent, scooped a handful of sand, and let it pour through his fingers. It reminded him of the fine golden hair of the lady Gudrid back in Greenland. She was Thorstein Eiriksson's widow and free to marry again. But he was here; and she, there. And he was not the only man to think her lovely. Regretfully he put aside the memory of her teasing smile and white fingers busy with her tools.

He wandered on down the beach. Others went with him. In the end it was Ketil who called his attention to the three distant humps on the sand.

"Quietly," Thorvald warned his men.

They drew their blades. As they crept down the beach, the rising sun sent their shadows, long and black, ahead of them.

The humps were boats of animal skin, pointed at both

ends, narrow and well made. "They look abandoned," Thorvald whispered. But they were upside down, and he was not a son of Eirik the Red for nothing. "Check beneath them."

Under each boat, sound asleep, were three beings in the shape of men. Their skin was copper-coloured. They looked half-starved, and were scantily clad, and they had only bows for weapons, cast down beside their sleeping forms. They carried no iron.

"Capture them," Thorvald mouthed.

It was done, but imperfectly. Of the nine, one escaped. Ketil bound the others. They spoke, but Thorvald did not understand them. "Skraelings," he named them with contempt. They would not even make decent slaves. You had to be able to speak to a slave to command him.

It was not the Northman's way to let captives go. His men were looking their question at him. He nodded and turned away. It was not fitting for Thorvald Eiriksson to end the lives of weaponless Skraelings.

They screamed, of course.

Ben moved restlessly against his pillow. The book slid off his bed and fell to the floor with a thud. He opened his eyes. The noise in his head was loud, siren-loud.

Skraeling screams. A hangover from his dream. That was all it was.

If the Vikings attacked first, who could blame them? Outnumbered, unsafe, the world around them full of dangers...

But eight men, bound and scared and unable to get away. Eight men, dead. It was the Skraelings who did that kind of thing, not the Vikings.

Ben had never really liked the part of the saga to do with Thorvald. He wished he hadn't read it again when he was so sleepy. And it hadn't even helped him find a name for his model. He said aloud, "I am Tor, Karlsefni's man, explorer and shipbuilder." Karlsefni's man, not Thorvald's. Things were different in Vinland when Karlsefni came.

He rubbed his eyes. The sound in his head faded, though it didn't quite go away. It was midnight. He had fallen asleep, reading, fully clothed, the light on, and without even brushing his teeth or seeing if Dad was home.

No wonder he felt as if something was seriously wrong.

TEN

"The fog's cleared," Dad said at breakfast the next morning. "Radio's calling for sunshine and no wind. Who's for another trip to L'Anse aux Meadows?"

"Is Ben going?" Keith asked.

Dad said sharply. "Ask him, not me."

"I'm busy anyway," Keith said.

"Then sure I'll come, Dad," Ben said, making a porridge dyke all the way across his bowl.

"I'm really getting tired of this," Dad said. "It's like living in a war zone. You two are *brothers*."

"Ben started it," Keith said. "He's mean to my friends. He's mean to—"

Dad pushed his chair away. "Enough," he said, and left the room.

"I don't care that you're not talking to me," Keith said when Dad was out of earshot. "Who needs you? I've got my friends."

Ben went to the sink and rinsed out his bowl.

"There's a poem goin' round Ship Cove. It's about your model. Wanna hear it?"

Unhurriedly, Ben filled the sugar bowl. Keith pressed both hands flat on the table and raised his voice a little. "It goes like this, see?

Stun ship so stun planned
She'll only sail good on a stand,
But what's even more grand
Is how she'll sink right on demand.

Everybody's sayin' it. Whatcha think, b'y, pretty good, huh?"

Ben looked out the window for a moment, as if thinking of nothing more than the blue sky outside. Then he headed slowly for his room. Once inside, though, he leaned his forehead against his closed door, and it was all he could do not to punch a hole through it.

Ross Colbourne had made up that rhyme, Ben was sure. But it had been Keith who made sure Ben heard it. Keith, the traitor.

Ben had never really wanted his brother to be a friend. But Keith had always been there to be looked after, a little kid who really looked up to his older brother. All that was gone. It was Ross Colbourne Keith turned to now. He had changed. Those boys had changed him.

"Ben?" Dad knocked on his door. Ben opened it.

"Keith's gone," Dad said. "Do you want to talk about it?"

Ben gazed steadily at his father. He didn't say anything.

"You're hurting him, Ben," Dad said carefully. "He needs you, and you're acting as if he isn't even there."

"Sure he needs me. Have you heard his little poem?"

"It's not worth listening to. Don't you see, Keith's just trying to get at you. To get through to you. He's trying to get your attention."

"He gets plenty of attention from Ross Colbourne's gang." Ben massaged his temples. The noise was starting up again. "Can't we just go?"

Dad sighed. "Do you remember where we left our backpacks?"

"Yours is in the kitchen. Mine's here."

"I'll pack us some grub."

With the model still sitting upright in its cradle, Ben rolled his sheepskin as small as possible and shoved it in his backpack. Then he added a block of wood to carve, and some tools, *The Vinland Sagas* and his book of Norse myths. He put the books in a large plastic bag to protect them against splashes on the way, then dropped them into the top of his backpack.

"I'll wait for you down at the dock, Ben," Dad called.

When the door slammed, Ben slipped across into Keith's bedroom. There was a box on the top shelf of Keith's closet. It had been full of Dad's old manuscripts, but Ben had taken a lot of the papers out and put them with others in his father's office. The empty place in the box was just big enough to hold his model. Ben had used it before, every time he had had to go out and leave the model behind. If Keith ever had tried to look for the little ship, he obviously hadn't imagined it could be in his own room, in a box he thought was full of Dad's things.

And if Keith couldn't find the model, neither could Ross Colbourne.

She'll never sail. Guarantee you she won't.

Ben wrapped the model in a sweater, placed the bundle carefully in the box and took it back to Keith's room.

When you lived with an enemy, you had to think like one.

♦

Down at *Viking's* dock Dad was chatting with Ed Jefferson, who was going at the ramshackle old fish stage with a scraper and paintbrush. A can of yellow paint stood open beside him. "Morning," Ben said, keeping his eyes on the paintbrush in Ed's huge, gnarled hand. From now on he wasn't giving anybody in Ship Cove the chance to look him in the eyes.

"Why don't you come over to the Viking site with us, Ed?" Dad said. "It's too nice a day to waste working."

"One day's good as another," Ed said, shrugging. "With cod the way it is, paintin's about all a man's good for."

Ben edged away down the dock. He dropped into *Viking*, where he fitted the oars to the oarlocks. Dad and Ed were still talking. He untied the painter, pushed away from the dock and began to row. The sun was warm on his head. The yellow swatch of colour on Ed's fish stage looked cheerful against the dull green shore. The oars felt good in his hands. For the first time in a long while there was no sound in Ben's head except the lapping of water against the hull.

When Dad left Ed and headed down the dock, Ben turned *Viking* around and brought her carefully back. "You all warmed up now?" Dad said, and dropped into the boat. "Okay. You've decided to go to Quarterdeck Cove. I'm cargo. It's all up to you."

Ben nodded to his father and yanked on the cord to start the engine. He had to do it twice before it responded. Dad didn't seem to notice. There were waggles in his wake as he steered for the bulge in Beak Point, but Dad didn't notice them, either. Now and then Ben looked toward the south, searching for the telltale shape of Quarterdeck Cove. Finally he saw it. He held his course, waiting to turn until it lined up with the very tip of Beak Point.

Now.

Viking headed inland. Ben hoped he would remember exactly when to cut the motor when he got to the cove. He hoped he could row close enough to that pyramid they were supposed to anchor under without banging into it. Above all he hoped he wouldn't hit a rock.

Dad hadn't cut the engine until the bumpy nose of the alligator headland was just to his right.

There.

Silence. The boat was still moving, but slower now. There were rocks ahead. Sweating, Ben fitted the oars to the oarlocks. "I'm going to backwater," he told his father. "I want to be able to see where I'm going."

"You're the captain," Dad said calmly.

"If you notice any rocks…" Ben began.

"Cargo doesn't have eyes," Dad reminded him.

All on his own. Okay. Ben backwatered several strokes, using slightly more push on the right oar to turn the boat to the left. The big pyramid was just ahead. Another stroke. *Viking* slid on. He shipped the oars. "Fenders," he muttered. He hung them over the side.

He was very close to the landing place now. He let the right oar slip into the water again and pushed on it, a very little. *Viking* angled toward the rocky pyramid. Too much. With the next stroke he pulled instead of pushing, again only barely. That was better. *Viking* was sliding into position.

He felt behind him for the stern grapnel. He had coiled the anchor line when they had come back from Quarterdeck Cove the last time. It wouldn't foul. He shipped the oar, turned around on the thwart, took hold of the anchor and threw. "Got it!" he shouted.

"Never doubted it for a minute," Dad said.

Viking bobbed. Ben fixed the line, then scrambled forward and threw the other grapnel.

Short.

Ben grimaced, hauled in the line and coiled it again. Dad didn't say anything. This time, Ben waited a moment before throwing. He pictured the grapnel going over that rock, hooking it securely. He pictured *Viking* moored snugly between the two rocks. He took a deep breath. This time the anchor hooked the rock.

"Fine job, cap'n," Dad said cheerfully. He gathered up the two knapsacks while Ben made sure the line was taut. "Now you can come over here on your own whenever you like."

Ben didn't trust himself to answer. The bog, the Viking lake, the Viking house, were really his now. He didn't have to stay in Ship Cove, stuck in the pink and purple house, waiting for Dad to be free to bring him here.

"As long as the weather's good, of course," Dad added hastily. "In Newfoundland, everything depends on the weather."

◆

Ben dropped his bundle of twigs on the floor of his Viking house, then scattered them carefully. He spread his sheepskin rug over the twigs and sat down on it with a grunt. Comfortable. Not a bit damp, either, with twigs between the sheepskin and the earth. Anyway, the foundation of the knoll was solid ground, not boggy.

He liked the smell of his house. For a while he just sat crosslegged on his rug breathing it in, the leathery smell of the sheepskin mingling with the spice of juniper and the loamy richness of the peat outside. The sunlight was dimly green and gentle, an almost magical blending of light and leaves. Roots silhouetted themselves against it, twisting like ropes rising into the world above. On the floor of his house a single plant grew, happily flowerless. Ben wanted to draw it against that surrealistic backdrop of light and roots, but he had forgotten his sketchpad.

The silence sang in his ears, a thin, high-pitched ringing that he had seldom heard before. It was the kind of silence you could hear only if you were absolutely alone. He listened to it gratefully, closing his eyes to hear it better, not letting himself even imagine any other sound for fear imagining it would make it come.

Dad was far away, tramping the bog. All the tourists were down at the reproduction sod huts by the bay. Some of them, maybe, would take the boardwalk and climb to the viewing platform on this knoll. They would look out dutifully, and then they would go on. They wouldn't realize that the Vikings were still up here in a way they no longer were in their abandoned sod houses down by the bay. There was too much noise down there for the Vikings. Too many people. Guides, reminding you that it was all history, over and done with. Signs telling you not to pick the flowers.

"By the knoll here is a sun-trap," Gudrid said. "As much as there is anywhere in Vinland. And the bog is fertile. We could grow peas here, maybe even cabbages."

"And the lake to water them with, if it should not rain," Astrid agreed eagerly.

Gudrid laughed. "You have been here eight months and can still imagine that? If a miracle happens and it does not rain, Astrid, the fog will water our garden for us."

Ben opened *The Vinland Sagas*. He deliberately turned to the section after Thorvald, starting at the very beginning of the Karlsefni expedition. He had read it before, of course, but never in his own Viking house. It would make all the difference reading it here.

Sixty men and five women made the journey from Greenland to Leifsbudir. They had seed for sowing and tools of all kinds, as well as livestock. The male animals, the bull particularly, grew strong and difficult to handle in this new country with its free and bountiful grazing. Summer passed into winter, and winter into summer. That was when, for the first time ever, the Skraelings came to Leifsbudir.

The Skraelings saw the bull, who bellowed at them threateningly. They had never seen a bull before. They were terrified and made for the longhouse and tried to get inside. But Karlsefni was wary, remembering Thorvald. He had the doors barred against them.

"They are afraid, husband," Gudrid said. "Listen to them. The bull is dangerous even to us, and we know how to handle it."

"I would trade with them," Karlsefni replied, "but allowing them into our home is different."

"Not even to save human lives?"

Karlsefni sniffed. "If they are smart enough to be human they will run away, not pound at our doors and wait for the bull to charge."

"Maybe they do not know that he will charge."

"Lady, they killed Thorvald," Tor put in.

Gudrid said impatiently, "One Skraeling arrow did that. One, Tor. And that was in revenge for the eight Skraelings Thorvald had ordered killed. In any case, it happened far away from here. These Skraelings likely had nothing to do with it."

Karlsefni shrugged. "Skraelings are all the same."

The bull charged. The Skraelings pleaded. Neither side could understand the other's language.

Ben closed the book. It was cool, after all, if you sat too long in a Viking house, shut away from the sun. And dim, too—much too dim, really, to read. He put the book into his backpack and listened. Still that silence. No way could there be anyone up on the knoll to watch where he came out of his secret house. He clambered up the earthen slope to the outside world and, just to be sure, cautiously pushed aside the juniper branch and peered out. But he was right, the top of the knoll was deserted. He scrambled out, straightened, shook off some juniper needles. The sun poured down, warming him instantly.

It was a pity he couldn't have a fire in his house. But he

could at least have more light. He would carve a candle-holder. He had brought a square block of pine for the purpose, left over from making the support cradle for his model. He decided to begin carving it down by his harbour.

He headed for the stairs at the far end of the knoll. The sun really was hot. The bog smelled of growing things, everything coming suddenly alive, the way yeast bubbled when Mom had added sugar and warm water to it, making bread. Ben could imagine the plants getting a jump-start on fall, the flowers turning quickly to berries, the berries ripening.

In Ottawa on a day like today he would probably be going to the community pool with Kevin and Peter. Ben missed swimming. He missed Kevin and Peter. He missed a lot of things he had once thought would always be there for him.

Skin Pond glittered before him, a sheet of blue glass. He crouched over his harbour, watching the water turn amber as he bent over it, clear right to the muddy bottom. Gently he touched a finger to its surface. Warm. Ripples spread as he took his finger away.

He could swim here. Right here in Skin Pond. The water was warm. It was fresh water, and clean. The Vikings had drunk it, certainly. There was nothing to stop him from swimming in it.

He thought about it. He didn't have his bathing trunks. But he was alone. Nobody would see if he swam in his underwear. If people did come, he could stay in the water till they were gone.

Never swim alone. The first rule you learned, when you took lessons. But the water wasn't that deep. He hadn't eaten recently, and anyway, he never got cramps. And he couldn't help it if he was alone up here, the only time the weather had ever been warm enough to take a swim.

He was always alone these days.

He pictured Kevin, diving a perfect jack-knife off the three-metre board. He pictured Peter blowing whale-like spouts, the way he had that summer three, maybe four years ago, when they had all just been little kids, and happy.

He stripped off his clothes and stepped in, exactly where he would moor his model.

The bottom was soft, but solid enough. Mud oozed through his toes. He took another step. The water was over his knees. Another. Deeper and deeper. It was like being stroked by cool silk. He wouldn't have believed it could feel so good.

He had had a blanket when he was very little. It was soft and smooth and cool and he always buried his face in it when Mom left the room after kissing him goodnight. In this water he remembered that blanket and wondered what had happened to it.

He was deep enough now, though the water was still not over his head. He put his face in the water, and began to swim.

"Good night, sleep tight, don't let the bedbugs bite."

She always said that, and then she always laughed, tucked his blanket around him, and kissed him three times.

"Once for you and once for me, and once for the grown-up you're going to be."

I'm going to swim across the lake, Ben thought. I'm going to swim as fast as I've ever swum in my life.

He did it. Then he did it again. After he did it a third time, he felt tired, and that was good. He turned over on his back and floated, eyes closed. The sun beat down, turning his closed eyelids red. He trod water, testing to see if he could touch bottom. He was about a quarter of the way out from the eastern side of the lake, but the water was only up to his neck. Ben grinned. He felt like a giant. One of the giants in the Norse myths, the one called Skrymir who had fooled Thor, maybe.

"*My name is Skrymir, and my glove alone is bigger than Valhalla. My cat is too big for Thor to lift, and my drinking horn reaches down to the sea.*"

The bottom of the lake was soft, squishing between his toes. Ben dragged his feet, enjoying the feeling. Slosh, suck, slosh, suck.

"*My foster mother is old age, who wins against all who wrestle with her. Only those who die first can—*"

"Ouch," Ben said.

He had stubbed his toe. He reached down to rub it, floundered, and went head over heels underwater. His hand scrabbled to push off the bottom and touched the thing he had stubbed his toe on. It felt…odd. Not like a root, or even a stone. He tugged, and it moved, but it was heavier than he expected, and he dropped it again. He was out of air. He came up, breathed hard, then duck-dived down again, open-eyed. But he had disturbed the mud, and the water was thick with it. He could see nothing. He went down a third time, searching with his fingers. This time he got it. To make sure, he closed both hands around it, then brought it to the surface.

He stared at what he'd found, and stared again.

It was an axe.

ELEVEN

The handle was wooden, black and water-logged. It went through the axe-head at a diamond-shaped join and stuck out a short distance on the other side. The axe-head was deeply pitted and corroded, but still looked formidable. Ben ran his finger along the blade. It wasn't sharp, but obviously it had been once. He was sure it was made of iron.

The whole thing looked very, very old.

"But it hasn't rusted," Ben muttered aloud, frowning. Didn't iron always rust in water? And wood rotted. So the axe couldn't have been in the lake that long. Unless...

"Peat mud," Grandpa's voice said suddenly in his brain. "All kinds of artifacts are found intact in peat, things that would rot to bits anywhere else. We found rust-free iron nails at the Viking site—a thousand years old, Ben, imagine it! And wooden things too, well preserved. Whenever we found anything, we kept it packed in wet peat moss in a plastic bag until we could get it to the lab."

Grandpa had said a lot more—stuff about oxygen and

acidic soil and bacteria—but Ben hadn't listened properly to that part. What mattered to him was that the archaeologists had found things the Vikings had actually used. It seemed a terrible pity that the most interesting things they found had been a cloak pin and a spindle whorl. A necklace or a drinking cup would have been really exciting. A sword or an axe would have been even better.

And now here he was with a very old axe in his hands.

Ben stared down at it. There was no way he could have found a real Viking axe. Things like that didn't happen to ordinary kids.

He dipped the axehead in water and brought it out again, just to see it glisten. Was that a pattern carved into the narrowest part of the handle, just by the blade? He squinted at it. Yes. It reminded him of the intersecting rings he had carved on the scrollboards of his model knarr.

It was a Viking pattern. And now he was seeing it again, or something very like it. A Viking pattern on an old axe handle.

Some kid who liked the Vikings must have bought the axe at a junk store and carved the rings on the handle. The kid had probably been a lot like Ben, somebody who played Vikings when he was little. And a woodcarver, too, of course. Maybe it had been that guy Brian who'd made the lighthouse village. Someone like that might easily have come over here and thrown the axe at a pretend Skraeling, and lost it in the lake.

If the axe were a real Viking artifact, Ben would have to turn it in at the visitors' centre. Then the archaeologists would come up to Skin Pond and tear the place apart, searching for more things the Vikings might have left here. The bog would be made off-limits to ordinary people. Dad wouldn't be able to come up here and tramp when he needed his elbow-room for the mind. Ben wouldn't be able to use his harbour or his Viking house.

It was a good thing, then, that it couldn't be a real Viking axe.

All the same, it was old, and someone had once liked it enough to decorate it. He should look after it as if it really were Viking. He would do what his grandfather had done, and cover it with peat moss and put it in a plastic bag. Every now and then he could take it out. Not to chop wood, of course. It wasn't sharp enough for that. But it would be just the thing to go with his Viking house.

He had a miniature Viking harbour, a model Viking ship, and now an imitation Viking axe. It was the best thing that had happened to him in a long, long time.

◆

Ben stayed up late that night making the sail for his model. He had cut a square from the back of an old wool shirt of his father's, one Dad had torn at the elbows. The shirt was a washed-out grey instead of the coloured stripes Ben would have preferred for the sail, but at least it was tightly woven and made of wool.

He cut the square twice as wide as the ship itself and rein-forced the edges by rolling the wool around thick twine. He wished he had a proper sailmaker's needle to stitch the roll, but there were only ordinary ones in Mom's old sewing box. Opening the box, Ben had a sudden vivid memory of his mother sewing a button on Keith's winter coat while he squirmed inside it. Everyone had been laughing, even Keith, but it was Mom's laughter Ben remembered, those funny, bub-bly little hiccups that always made him think of the champagne bottle Dad uncorked at midnight on New Year's.

Their first Yule in Vinland was over. It had been a week of feast-ing and storytelling, of ham-handed Ulf playing his bone flute with astonishing delicacy, of Karlsefni and Gudrid leading the dance. Now a New Year's quiet lay on Leifsbudir, deep as the snow.

In the firelight, men were silent, playing at hnefiafl or whit-
tling or simply lying on their sleeping platforms remembering peo-
ple and places far away. Tor was thinking of his mother, who had
cried when he had left Iceland with Karlsefni, and of little Sigurd,
who had been too young to realize that Tor might never come
back. More than four years had gone by. Sigurd would be nine
now.

He had worshipped Tor the way little boys do the bigger ones
who now and then are kind to them. And Tor had made it a prac-
tice to be kind to Sigurd. It pleased his mother, and, truth be told,
it pleased himself.

He had loved the boy. He had loved his mother. It seemed
incomprehensible, sometimes, that they were out of his life. He
was Karlsefni's man, and he was Gudrid's man, but in the New
Year's silence after the meal he felt as cut off as if he had gone with
the dead to Hela's realm in Nifelheim, instead of only across an
ocean to Vinland.

"I have a secret to tell you." It was Gudrid, kneeling by his
sleeping platform, smiling. "Tor, I am with child. Your lord knows
about his son, but only he so far. I wanted you to know, because
I dreamed last night that you would protect him one day when no
one else could. I wanted you to know."

Joy lightened Tor's heart. "I will protect him," he vowed. "I
will be his man, as I am Karlsefni's and your own."

Once the sail was edged, Ben began making twine loops
to attach the top of it to the wooden yardarm. That was how
the sail would be raised and lowered, by hauling the yardarm
up the mast, the sail going with it. He was sitting hunched
over the kitchen table, surrounded by scraps of cloth and
twine, when his father came out of his bedroom. "You should
be in bed, Ben," Dad said. "It's past midnight."

Ben blinked at him. Sewing needles and champagne bot-
tles and a smoke-filled longhouse swam before his eyes. "Just

going," he muttered, scooping the scraps into a garbage bag. He hadn't realized how tired he was. It was bad, having to wait until Keith went to bed to feel right about working on the model.

"Neat sail," Dad commented. He smiled a little. "That old shirt of mine hasn't looked so good in years. Do you have to make rope loops for the bottom, too?"

Surely Dad knew that. "You let the sail billow out at the bottom. A rope at each corner. They showed it in the visitors' centre in L'Anse aux Meadows."

"That's right, I remember now." He paused. "You'll be launching her pretty soon, I expect. Keith might like to help you."

Ben got to his feet. "Keith can help his *friends*. They're probably hard at work on another rhyme for when the model's done. Let Keith help *them*."

"Ben, give him a chance. He's made a few mistakes, but so have you. Can't you just forget everything and start over?"

"From where?"

Lorne looked at him sadly. "You lug the past around like a boulder on your back. It's heavy, b'y, too heavy to live with all the time. Why don't you just drop it?"

"I don't know what you're talking about."

"Don't you?" He looked his son square in the face. "This isn't Florida, Ben."

"I'm going to bed." Steadily. Carefully.

Dad pretended to laugh. "Climate's completely different, for one thing. For another—look, Ben, you know what I'm trying to say. Ross's gang isn't—"

Ben stopped him. "Ross's gang isn't anything to do with anything," he said. "And it's after midnight, and I'm tired, and I want to go to bed."

"Goodnight, then," Dad said. He sounded discouraged. "Ben..."

"What?"

"I'm not very good at helping you, but it doesn't mean I don't want to."

"I don't need any help. Goodnight."

Tomorrow, if Keith left early enough, he'd finish the rigging. With any luck at all, the little ship would be entirely finished by tomorrow night. The next day, weather permitting, he would take her over to the bog. And then...

She would cross the lake, her own little sea. It would be a voyage worthy of exuberant crowds cheering from the shore, but there would only be Ben to see.

He shut his bedroom door. He wished the model were in his own room where he could look at it and touch it, instead of in the box in Keith's closet. Without the model beside him, he felt weighed down, as if it had all been too much for him, as if everything was too much.

Shoulders slumped, he flopped onto the bed. He was wearing sweatpants and a shirt; they were as comfortable as pajamas. He tugged a blanket over himself and fell asleep at once, a true falling, heavy as a stone dropping through water into a soft ooze where things lay forever unchanged.

◆

The model was finished by the middle of the next afternoon. With shaking fingers, Ben placed it in its cradle beside his bed, then stood back to inspect his labour. He examined it from the stern and then from one side, and then he crawled onto his bed and pressed his back into the wall to examine it from the other. He squeezed between the window and his bedside table and looked at the model from bow to stern. Then he went back and re-examined it from stern to bow. He blew on his fingers to warm them, as if it were the cold that was causing them to shake, then carefully untied the yardarm. Gentle as a mother, he raised it to the mast-head.

The sail hung slack in the motionless air. He tied down the two corner ropes, his fingers still oddly trembly, then bent over and blew against the wool. The sail billowed outward. He stood back quickly, while the sail still had some life in it. He took one of the tiny oars between his forefinger and his thumb and carefully pushed it through the oar-hole, then leaned it against the little bench he had placed inside. Then he stood back again. Sunlight from his window lit the ship like a spotlight.

He had never made anything this good, never in his life.

His work.

Only his.

"Looks like it's done," Keith's voice said.

Ben whirled, instinctively shielding the model. Keith was standing in the doorway. "Where'd you come from?" Ben shot out.

"The living room." Sarcastically. "And before that, the front door. And—"

"You were up on the headland," Ben said tightly. "I watched you go."

"You always watch."

"You said you'd only be a sec, Keith." Melissa's voice, out in the living room. So she was here too. How could the two of them have come in so quietly that Ben hadn't even heard them?

"How long's it take to find a fish-net, b'y?"

There was no mistaking that cool, bored drawl. "You brought Ross here?" Ben hissed at Keith.

Keith called casually over his shoulder, "Ben's model's done, Ross. Want to see?"

He had told them about Florida. He had let them into the house. And now he was inviting them into Ben's room. Ben's breath whooshed out and in.

"The one that won't sail?" Coolly. "Needs some help yet, do he?"

"Get out," Ben told Keith. His back was to his bedside table. He could feel the model on it, feel it, though no part of it touched his body. A door slammed. Dad? No, there'd been no noise of a car driving up. Jimmie and Dave, then, come to help Ross out. Five against one.

Ben looked at Keith, and it was as if his brother and he were alone together on a wide black road that connected only them. Noise erupted in his head, drumroll and siren, loud, loud. Dusk was falling, fog blotting out everything but the book open on his lap and the steering wheel beside him. He blinked the fog away, lurched forward.

Keith backed away, his eyes huge. "Ben?" he said.

Melissa appeared suddenly in the doorway behind Keith. "Go get your net, b'y." She gripped Keith's shoulder, turned him around and gave him a little push. Not once, not for a single moment, did she take her eyes off Ben's.

Ben blinked at her. He stopped moving forward. His fists dropped. He blinked again.

"Ross got tired of waitin'," Melissa explained, though he hadn't said a word. She looked grown up all of a sudden, tall, almost stern.

It was all Ben could do to hold in his trembling. The noise in his head dulled slowly. Melissa waited. An eternity passed.

"My model's done," Ben got out at last, every word hurting. "Do you want to see?"

"No." She pursed her lips, then added slowly, "You haven't got the sense God give to a cat, Ben Elliott. You been a jerk ever since you got here. But here and there you been decent to me, so I'm gonna warn you. Knock off with the high and mightiness. Just lay off, my son."

He stared at the floor. His head throbbed. He wanted to

rub it, but he wouldn't, not with her there.

"Ross and the others...look, nobody never jerked you around, not yet. But if you does one more thing..." He didn't raise his eyes from the floor. Her voice went tight. "Okay. Here it is, plain. Look out to your own self, and look out to that dumb model of yours. Got me?"

Why did she think she had to warn him about something he already knew?

"You ready, Liss?" came Keith's voice, still sounding a little scared.

"Keith," Ben said steadily to the floor.

"What?" Hostile.

"I didn't mean to..." But he had meant to. He pressed his lips together and didn't say another word.

They left then. He waited for a moment, then went over to the door and shut it. I'm tired, he thought numbly.

After a long moment he turned to look at his model again. The sunlight had gone. The model seemed so lifeless that he went over to touch it, to reassure himself it had not changed.

"I'll take you to Skin Pond tomorrow," he whispered to the little ship.

He would leave the model in his Viking house. She would be safer there. Everything that mattered to him would be together then: the model, the axe, the house, the harbour.

"Look out to your own self, and look out to that dumb model of yours."

He still hadn't named his ship. With hands that shook, he pulled *The Vinland Sagas* from his bookshelf and took it over to his bed.

TWELVE

*G*udrid sat by the doorway near the cradle of her son. Her hair hung in a single corn-silk braid over one shoulder. She was attaching the soapstone weight to her spindle, the autumn sun gleaming on the comb and scissors that dangled from the front of her grey apron. She scooped a handful of freshly combed wool from the pile at her feet and made ready to spin. Behind her the wood-smoke from the longhouse hearth combined with the good cooking smell of barley porridge. Her stomach growled loudly.

"Are you hungry, my lady?" Tor asked from the bench on the other side of the cradle.

She smiled ruefully. "I am always hungry these days."

"Unas!" Tor called through the door of the longhouse. "Your lady Gudrid needs food."

"It's the babe's fault," Unas said, bringing her a bread roll. "You eat for him as well as you, lady, and he is a greedy little thing."

She dropped a kiss on the sleeping child's head, then went back to her work. Young Snorri was aptly named, Tor thought, smiling to himself as the little one bubbled away contentedly in his sleep.

While Gudrid ate, he let his eyes roam the grassy compound inside the palisade. Freyda was feeding the geese and Astrid was hanging fish onto the drying racks, but there was no sign of any of the men. He supposed they were readying themselves for the Skraelings' daily trading visit, which was now always handled outside the palisade.

"It is a nuisance, that palisade," Gudrid said, seeing what he was looking at. "I miss the views we used to have. And I hate the feeling that we are prisoners in our own settlement."

Tor wished Nils could have heard his lady say this. He would not then so readily speak of the palisade as being Gudrid's fault.

"Still," she went on, "if Snorri and I are to be prisoners, Tor, I'd rather you were our jailer than anyone else."

"Lady!" Tor protested. "I am no jailer. You can go where you please. I am only taking my turn protecting you and the babe while the Skraelings are nearby."

Laughter bellowed from outside the gate. "That's Ulf for sure," she said, "and Bjorn too, by the sound of it. I hope they're not drinking."

"Not likely," Tor said. "A man does not deal with Skraelings on a belly full of mead." Particularly not Skraelings who were being cheated in trade, he added to himself. And there were more of the strangers every day, more of them offering their valuable furs, more of them hungrily eyeing the iron weapons of the Northmen. After all this time, none of them could recognize any language but hand-signals.

Tor turned his eyes to the baby, whose golden curls were lifting in the breeze to show the pink scalp beneath. "There's a cool edge to the wind," he told Gudrid. "Perhaps the child would be the better for a blanket behind his head."

She laughed at him. "Let him be," she said. "The sun is warm. Let him enjoy it while it lasts."

The baby whimpered, and his blue eyes opened. She put down her spindle and ran her finger gently down the infant's cheek. "Sleep, Karlsefni's son. It is too soon to wake. Sleep."

He didn't cry, but he didn't sleep, either. And no wonder. The noise outside the palisade was louder now, and not so pleasant. Tor guessed that the Skraelings had come. Karlsefni's deep bellow could be heard above the rest of the confusion. "Drink your milk!" he shouted jovially. "Drink, my Skraelings, and we may decide the sun is too warm to kill you today."

"I wish he would take more thought for the future," Gudrid whispered to herself. "Milk for furs, and watered milk at that."

Tor couldn't help agreeing. The Skraelings had not known milk until Karlsefni had given it to them. "A babe's drink," he had announced at the evening meal, the first day he had offered it. "No wonder they love it." And every day they had come back for more.

"We will run short of milk," Gudrid had warned her husband in Tor's hearing.

"When we do, my Gudrid, we shall give them water and tell them it is milk."

"They aren't stupid, husband."

"Are they not? Then we shall water the milk, a little more each day, and see how long it takes them to notice."

The noise outside the palisade changed again. Now it had an ugliness that Tor had not heard before. There came a sudden clash of metal: men pulling their blades. He jumped to his feet, sword in his hand. "Go inside, lady," he commanded. Gudrid scooped the baby into her arms and disappeared into the longhouse.

The gate swung inward, revealing a knot of Northmen, their backs to the palisade. Karlsefni was the only one who faced the longhouse, protected by the men in front of him. He entered the compound alone, latching the gate behind him.

Tor took three steps forward, then waited. Guarding the long-

house, not the palisade, was his duty. Karlsefni hurried toward him. "What's the matter?" Tor asked.

"They don't like the milk. They have drawn weapons." Karlsefni called into the longhouse, "Quick, wife. What might the Skraelings like instead of milk?"

Gudrid stuck her head out the door. Scanning her husband's face, she bit her lip and said, "Our linens. The red cloth especially."

"Get the women to cut some up."

"How much?"

"Fifty strips. Not too wide. Long enough for a man to wrap around his head."

She nodded silently. He was back through the gate before she could enter the house.

Tor waited, his sword ready. The Skraelings had discovered they were being cheated with watered milk. How soon before they learned the value of a scrap of red cloth?

Red cloth. Ben blinked. He was not in Leifsbudir. He was in his bedroom in a pink and purple house at three in the afternoon, and only fifteen minutes had passed since Keith and Melissa had left.

He was staring at a page of *The Vinland Sagas*. The words wouldn't stay still.

It had been his job to look after her. His job to see that her little son came to no harm.

Look after a woman long dead, and her little son too? What was he thinking of? It was the Tor game playing itself out a little more vividly than usual, that was all. Imagination, nothing more.

The book shook in his hands. No wonder the words wouldn't stay still.

His job to look after her. His job to keep her little son from harm.

He thought of Keith. He had almost pounded him out.

He'd deserved it, of course, but—he'd been so surprised. Ben had never seen him like that before, eyes so big in that pale, frightened face.

Her little son.

Read. Don't think. Just read. You're looking for a name for the model.

A name for the model.

The words settled down. For about six pages he knew what he was reading. Then he came to the place where Gudrid was sitting by the doorway near her baby. Ben nodded. That was right; he had been there, sitting beside her. She'd been spinning and eating a bread roll and stroking the baby's cheek. And he had wanted to tuck a blanket around the baby's head because the wind was cool. And Gudrid had laughed at him. And then the men outside had drawn their swords.

He caught himself up. He hadn't been there. Gudrid hadn't laughed at him. He'd imagined it all. Because in the saga something else altogether had happened at the time Gudrid sat by the doorway near the cradle, some weird supernatural thing with another woman appearing and then vanishing. The business of being on guard and the cool wind and the Norsemen drawing their swords—all of it had been his own invention.

But it hadn't felt like invention. Never before had the Tor game felt so real.

◆

"Finnborg is dead."

Gudrid was stooping, straightening the loom weights that the baby, a year old now and always getting into mischief, had tangled. She straightened, looking into Karlsefni's face, then Tor's. "How?" she asked.

"His own sword," Karlsefni answered. His face was white with fury. "He was asleep on watch. One of the Skraelings took

the sword, then killed him."

"And the Skraeling?"

"Caught and killed. Others saw."

Gudrid's face went distant. "Three canoes on a beach," she murmured, like one farseeing. "Nine Skraelings, then eight dead men, and one to spread the tale. Iron and blood mixing to no purpose. Thor's hammer cast, and no going back."

"Gudrid!" Karlsefni said irritably. "This is now, not then. We must plan what to do."

"What would you have me do?" she asked aloud, but Tor was not fooled by her surface calm. Tor wondered that Karlsefni couldn't see.

"Tell the women to make food," Karlsefni ordered.

Food first, then drink, then talk; the women in shadows, listening. It was always the way, Tor thought, Old World or New.

"As my lord bids," Gudrid said. She stood very straight, then whirled away.

Tor followed her. He couldn't help it. "What, lady? What are you thinking?"

The words burst out of her. "I am thinking that I am glad Finnborg has no wife. I am thinking that there will be war between us and the Skraelings. I am thinking that it is as well our ships are ready to sail whenever we need them."

"Are you farseeing this? It is not just fear? You know that we will have to leave Vinland?"

She clenched her fists, then carefully released them. "It is not just fear. Go away, Tor. I have work to do."

The men ate. They drank. They talked. "The Skraelings will come again," Karlsefni said, "and in much greater numbers. We must be ready for them. This is what we must do."

The women listened. The sheep and cattle would be herded into a secret clearing so the Skraelings could not harm them. Ten men would make themselves conspicuous cutting trees in the for-

est near the lake, a draw for Skraeling attack. When the Skraelings came pouring toward the woodcutters, with the lake on one side and the woods on the other, Karlsefni's other men would close in from behind.

"They will be between two prongs of a pincer," Karlsefni said. "They will not escape."

He began assigning men. Tor was chosen for the woodcutting party, with Ulf Njordsson in command. The rear attacking force was to be under Karlsefni. There would be one man only at the longhouse: Rollo, who had been wounded in the lung on a raiding party ten years before and could never breathe quietly thereafter. He was a strong warrior, but he was one who had listened most avidly to Nils's gossip about Gudrid. He did not approve of Gudrid, and Tor knew she did not like him.

Gudrid listened quietly, and when her lord's drinking bowl was empty, she refilled it. But Tor saw her face, looking at Rollo.

"The Skraelings will not escape," Karlsefni finished confidently. "Did you say something, wife?"

"Would you have some dried grapes, my lord? They are very sweet."

"I said, did you want any dessert? Ben?"

Ben blinked at his father. "What?"

"Dessert. I don't usually have to ask you twice."

Dad was holding out a tray of brownies that Mrs. Goudie had made for them.

"No, thanks."

"But you love brownies."

"I'm not hungry."

"You didn't eat much of your chicken."

Ben didn't remember any chicken. He remembered sour beer in a wooden bowl, a grainy porridge that needed a lot more salt, and a horrible, greasy kind of meat.

"I'll eat his brownie," Keith volunteered, without looking at Ben.

"There's lots for both of you," Dad said firmly. "Ben?"

There didn't seem to be much choice. Ben took a brownie.

"A box came in the mail for you today, Ben," Dad said, after a moment. "It's in your bedroom."

"What is it?"

"Books. I ordered them from Toronto. You've been missing having new ones to read. I thought..."

Ben smiled, genuinely pleased. "That's great, Dad. Thanks a lot."

"I told the bookstore person what kind of thing you and Kevin and Peter used to read. They sent the newest ones like that, plus the latest award-winners, and a couple I thought of myself."

"Can I go and look at them now?" he asked as eagerly as he could. He had hoped, when Dad had said books, they might have been about woodworking or the Vikings, things like that. But Dad had tried. And he *was* grateful.

"Finish your dinner first."

"Did you get me anything?" Keith asked jealously.

"A whole new set of Lego."

"Wow!"

"But it hasn't come yet. A couple more days, the store said. Hey, boyos, there's a great Monty Python movie on TV tonight."

"Snakes," Keith said, grimacing. "Ugh."

"*Monty* Python, Keith," Dad said with a little snort of amusement. "Well, maybe it wouldn't be your cup of tea. How about you, Ben?"

Ben didn't want to watch movies. He felt as if he'd been watching them all day in his head. "I want to look at my new books."

"Did you see the weather report for tomorrow, Dad?" Keith asked.

Ben began clearing plates. Dad seemed not to notice that he hadn't eaten any of the brownie. He was answering Keith. "Continuing fine, the radio said. Got special plans?"

"Ross's dad said we could take their boat out whale-watching, if it's fine. We saw a pod of humpbacks off the cape today, near the Onion. Six of 'em, easy—it was great. Ross says they sing sometimes. He's heard 'em."

The Onion. Ben took a relieved breath. That was the rock at the northern end of the cape: the opposite direction to Quarterdeck Cove. If Ross's gang went there, he could take his model to Skin Pond without any witnesses.

Dad said, "Maybe Ben would like to go whale-watching with you fellows, Keith."

"Who cares?" Keith said.

"No way," Ben said loudly at the same moment.

Dad closed his eyes. Then he opened them again. "Do you know how much your mother would have hated this? We used to be a team. What's happened to us?"

For a moment there was dead silence in the kitchen. Suddenly Dad scraped his chair back. Without looking at them he said, "I'm going for a walk. I don't care how you divide up the work, but when I get back, this kitchen had better be tidy. And if I find even the slightest trace of blood on the floor—"

Neither Ben nor Keith said anything the whole time he was gone. But when Dad got back, the kitchen was tidy, and there was no blood on the floor, or anywhere else.

◆

Spread out one beside the other, the new books completely covered Ben's bedroom floor, his bed, and the desk as well. There were dozens of them, fantasy and mystery and adventure and just plain fiction. Two, Ben guessed, were Dad's own choices: a Kevin Major novel that took place in Newfoundland, and one by Sarah Ellis called *Next-Door Neighbours*, whose title Dad must have seen as a message especially for Ben. Only one was non-fiction, and it wasn't about woodcarving, but about gardening in a northern climate.

After he had spread the books out he called his father to admire them, and then, very carefully, he put them away in his bookcase, neatly lined up with no space between them. He was tired enough after that to go right to bed.

He almost expected to dream: something more about Gudrid and the baby, or Karlsefni and the Skraelings. But if he did, he had no recollection of it. He slept late, waking only when he heard Dad and Keith talking in the kitchen. He should have felt rested, but he didn't. For at least ten minutes he lay in bed without moving. The model on the table beside him had to be taken over to the Viking house, but he couldn't do that until he was sure Keith was gone.

He got dressed, then waited to leave his room until he heard the door slam behind Keith. Just to be safe, he wrapped the model in his sweatshirt and put it in his backpack before leaving his room. The kitchen was full of sunlight. Dad was sitting at the table, sipping coffee and making a list. "I'm going to St. Anthony's for groceries," he said when Ben came in. "You want to come?"

He, too, said it "Snantny's," Ben noticed.

"No, thanks. I'm going up on the bog."

"Well, you've got a good day for it," Dad said. "I'd come too, if we weren't out of just about everything. Anyway, I've promised Ed a lift to town. You're not going to launch the model today, are you?"

"No," Ben lied. Or maybe it wasn't a lie. He didn't know, for sure. He still didn't have a name for her, after all.

"That's good. I'd hate to miss that. She's a beautiful piece of work, Ben."

Dad was the only person who had seen the model; the only person who had wanted to. "Thanks," Ben said, his voice low.

Dad gathered up his list, checked his pockets and looked at his watch. "Got to run," he said. "Be careful in *Viking*, Ben. Say hello to the bog for me."

He was gone.

◆

Ben was just about to drop into *Viking* when it happened again.

"Be careful," Gudrid said. She said it to all the men—all but Rollo, who stood importantly beside her in the longhouse door.

Tor didn't like having to leave her in Rollo's care. But his lord had assigned him to be innocently logging when the Skraelings came against them. They were all sure it would be today. The Skraeling thief had died yesterday, and the Skraelings had shown years ago with Thorvald that they were not good at waiting for revenge.

Most of the other women were huddled against the longhouse. Unas stood on Gudrid's other side, Snorri squirming in her arms. "Remember you have a son, my lord," Gudrid said to Karlsefni. "He needs a father."

"He will have one. The Skraelings cannot win. Animals do not win battles against thinking men."

"We cannot stay here much longer," she said.

Karlsefni looked at her queerly, then waved his men back. But Tor hovered as close as he dared, pretending to examine the fish drying from the rack near the longhouse. He wanted to hear.

"Is this the foreknowledge singing in you?" Karlsefni demanded.

"We have made mistakes in Vinland," she answered.

"What mistakes?" He was very serious now.

"Thorvald made the first. You will make another today."

"We must fight the Skraelings, wife. We have no choice."

"No choice now." She turned away.

"Meaning?"

She faced him again. Tor could see her hands twisting together, as if that would somehow make Karlsefni understand. "They are not animals, husband. They are what we are. They want what we want, need what we need. We should have dealt with them differently."

"Gudrid, there is no free land anywhere in the world except here. Vinland is the future for all Northmen. We must fight to keep it."

"There were other ways to keep it, once," she said. "We did not have to fight the Skraelings. There is room in Vinland for us both."

"They do not think so."

"Not any more."

"We will win today," Karlsefni said firmly.

"Yes."

"And after that, Vinland will be ours."

She threw her arms around him. "No."

"No," Tor echoed. He had heard the truth in Gudrid's voice. Vinland would never be theirs, never.

It was like a movie, suddenly shut off. Ben stood there, blinking down at *Viking*. "No," he muttered. The Tor game was getting too real. He didn't like it any more. "No."

"That's what I thought ya said," a voice drawled.

Slowly Ben turned his head. Ross Colbourne stood on the dock, eyes narrow as knife blades. "I asked polite," he said.

"I didn't ... what did you ... ?" Ben stumbled to a halt.

"Frig if I cares. Who wants to see a boat that can't even sail?"

Ben blinked dazedly at him. Ross turned away. Over his shoulder he said, "It was only Lissa, see, sayin' as how you wanted to show it off. Dumb girls, goin' on and on at ya, ya gotta shut 'em up somehow."

He swaggered off.

The model. *That* was what Ross had asked to see.

"I didn't hear you!" Ben called after him, suddenly desperate.

But Ross was out of sight around the corner of the fishing stage, and made no reply.

THIRTEEN

The light in his Viking house was gentle as dusk, though it was barely noon. Instinctively Ben had come here first, bypassing his Viking harbour. It was a perfect day for sailing, the wind out of the west and just strong enough to send the model skimming over the rippled pond, but he wasn't ready. *She* wasn't ready. She needed naming.

A real Viking would know what to name her.

The plastic bag containing his axe was on an earthen shelf he had chiselled out of the hillside. He fumbled at the twist-tie. The peat moss was still sodden, he noted with satisfaction. The axe was cold and wet.

He lifted it out of its mossy bed, swinging it two-handed through the green-tinted sunlight of his Viking house.

Tor swung his axe, and in barely half a dozen blows the young spruce tree toppled. He wished he had another axe with him, not his good shipbuilding one. He had never used this one as a weapon. He did not not wish to begin today.

He was a hunter, a shipbuilder, Karlsefni's man and his lady's guard. He had been on raids. He had seen men killed; he had inflicted his own share of injuries. He was, after all, a Northman. But he did not want to see men's blood on this axe that had made so many beautiful things. He did not want to be cutting down a tree with it for no other purpose than to give him a reason to be here, bait for the Skraeling attack that would certainly come soon.

"There is little honour in this," Nils said, almost as if he had read Tor's mind. He grunted as he shoved his own tree so that it toppled to the ground beside Tor's. "It is not the Northman's way to wait like a tethered goat for the wolves to come."

Bjorn heard him and came over, leaving his own tree barely notched. The leader of their ten-man band, Ulf Njordsson, shoved his axe in his belt and followed him. "The Skraelings are not wolves," Ulf demurred lazily. "And only one of them that I've ever seen is worthy of a Northman's blade."

"Their leader, you mean," Tor said. "The tall one who does all the talking."

"If you can call that jabber talking."

Nils laughed. "Astrid names him Ovaegir. She likes him."

"Ovaegir." Ulf smiled gently. "He has a name, then."

"He was the one who first noticed that we were watering the milk," Bjorn put in. "He has some skill with the knife, too."

Ulf nodded. "Ovaegir. I am glad to know his name."

Ovaegir, Ben thought. It was a name, though not the one he wanted. He had hoped when he took the axe in his hands that it might put him in the mood for the Tor game. If he pretended he was a Viking shipbuilder, then he might think of the perfect name for his own little model knarr. But Tor had not been shipbuilding. He had been readying himself for battle. And Ben hadn't done anything to make the Tor game start. It had happened on its own. Again. And it hadn't felt like a game at all. Ben had no control over Tor any more; he hardly believed that he was even imagining him.

With icy hands he lowered the axe to his side. Then, very carefully, he put the axe back in the bag, mushed the peat moss around it and laid it on its shelf.

He could try going through *The Vinland Sagas* again, or the book of Norse myths, to see if somehow he'd missed the perfect name. But he knew he hadn't. The only names in the sagas and the myths belonged to other ships and other people. This was his ship. Her name would have to come from his mind, or nowhere.

He undid his backpack and got out the wrapped-up bundle. Slowly he unwrapped it, then placed the little ship lengthwise in her cradle on the earth in front of him. He stepped the mast but left the sail furled. Then he sat back on his heels and waited for the name to come.

Dappled green light danced on the little knarr, magical, timeless.

"She's exquisite," Mom said. *"Look at her, Ben. She's the best you've ever made."*

You didn't notice the height of prow and stern so much from this angle. Even the cross made by mast and yardarm were foreshortened. What stood out here, in the strange pale light of his Viking house, was the wide expanse of unstained pine boards curving up and out, like cupped white hands.

It was hard to imagine boards this thin separating people and animals from the lash of a northern ocean.

"There's no point thinking like that," Mom said. *"The planks don't separate your knarr from the sea; they connect her to it. You could make a ship out of plate steel and she could still never be stronger than the sea. But make her light and flexible, and she'll ride the waves instead of fighting them."*

"What if she's driven up against the rocks?"

"You didn't design her to do that, did you? You designed her to sail."

"But ships do wreck, Mom." Light, flexible, beautiful ships came flying over the sea only to be torn to pieces by the brutal shore.

"An unlucky wind, an unlucky shore, an unlucky iceberg, anything can sink. That doesn't matter. What matters is how she sails."

He lifted the model from her cradle, closing his eyes the better to feel her, wood stripped to the root of its strength and as supple as fine leather. Warm hands seemed to cup his own, the same hands that had held his when he had first taken up the woodcarver's chisel, the hands that had guided his strokes with the plane, that had shown his how to tap along a piece of pine in the lumber yard and know if it would do what he needed. *"There now, you see? She will sail, Ben. Whatever happens to her in the end, she will sail."*

He opened his eyes and looked at his Viking knarr. It was fragile and beautiful, and it was made Mom's way—a ship made to sail, not founder.

"Frances Torland Elliott," Ben said aloud, his mother's name. He didn't mean to say it, but somehow it came out anyway. The back of his neck started to prickle, the way it always did when he had found the right name for one of his models.

"Frances," he said. His voice shook.

It was the model's true name. It had been her true name all along.

◆

On the flat rock on the western side of Skin Pond across from his harbour, Ben bent over the *Frances*, sitting in her cradle in front of him. Carefully he untied the strings that held the furled sail to the yardarm and pulled on the halyard until the sail was fully up and open. He licked his finger to feel the wind. Still out of the west. A following wind for her maiden voyage, Ben told himself happily. You couldn't ask for better.

He made the sail's corner ropes fast to each side of the hull, keeping the sail square. The steering oar went in last, the blade parallel to the keel. He lashed it, using a knot that would undo quickly if he needed to go to the rescue of the little ship. But the wind was steady and just the right strength; he did not believe for a moment that he would have to swim after the model.

One at a time he pushed the oars through their holes. He would leave them out just for the model's first contact with the water, a kind of ceremonial dunking. In his backpack was a Mars bar. Ben got it out, remembering the one Dad had called Viking treasure the first time they'd come to Quarterdeck Cove. He unwrapped it carefully, then broke it into three pieces. The gods expected their due when Viking ships were launched. He dropped one of the pieces of chocolate into the water, saying, "Aegir, god of the sea, protect this ship." A second piece. "Ran, wife of Aegir, protect this ship." The last. "Njord of the wind and the sea, protect this ship."

There, Ben thought. That's done.

He picked the model up in both hands, holding her high. "I name you *Frances*," he said loudly. Then he put her in the water. His mind flashed orders at him: keep her broadside to the wind, get the oars safely stowed, make everything tidy. But for a long moment he only crouched there, looking at her.

There she was, his *Frances*, in Viking waters at last. Floating. Free to sail. Free.

He stowed the oars. Tremulously, he turned her bow away from land to face her home harbour away across this inland sea. "Sail," he said, and gave her a gentle push.

Briefly she drifted, then the wind caught her sail. It filled. The little ship began to move more purposefully, setting a straight course for the harbour. Water rippled around her bow.

She was sailing.

Ben stood up, watching her scud away from him. The wind was right. The course was right. The speed was right. Everything was right.

I should go to the other side, Ben thought. I should be waiting for her when she gets there.

But he couldn't move.

Some oak, some pine, Mom's training, and Ben. Life from all that. Life.

There had been a parking lot in Florida, an Ontario car parked there alone in the foggy dusk. There had been an eleven-year-old boy reading in the car while his mother was in the store. There had been things happen then—terrible things.

And even after all that, there could be life.

A glitter lay on the little ship, a brightness of sun and lake water. Ben dashed his hand against his eyes. Tears spilled out.

"An unlucky wind, an unlucky shore, an unlucky iceberg, anything can sink. That doesn't matter. What matters is how she sails."

The *Frances* was sailing, and there was only him to see.

◆

"They are coming." The whisper went up and down the line of men. Briefly, one after another, axes ceased to chop, then started again, industriously.

"Are you ready to prove to the Skraelings that this is our place?" Ulf demanded softly.

Our place. Tor thought of Gudrid. She would take issue with that idea. But he nodded with the rest and swung his axe hard against the tree. A Skraeling body, next time. They had killed Finnborg. They wanted the Northmen's weapons. They would not take milk or red cloth for an answer now.

He allowed himself a single swift glance to his left. Scrub forest in the distance, blanketing the knoll; then the cleared path they'd made to the lake where he would put Snorri's miniature knarr when the boy was a little older. The Skraelings were approaching openly along the lakeshore as if for their usual trading exchange, but even from here, Tor could see the difference. There were more of them. Their weapons were more in evidence, and there was something more purposeful than usual and insolently aggressive about the way they walked. They were not heading for the palisade, either, but for the line of men busily logging and apparently unaware of them. Their leader was the one called Ovaegir.

"I think we will not wait any longer for them," Ulf said when the Skraelings were between the knoll and the lake, and Karlsefni's hidden men were behind them. "I think we will go and meet them now."

◆

Pounding footsteps.

Ben had heard them before. For two years feet had pounded inside his skull, steel-toed boots coming out of the fog to get him. But this was different. This was no memory.

His stomach clenched. He turned his eyes away from the *Frances*. He knew exactly who he would see, running down the boardwalk from Quarterdeck Cove.

Ross Colbourne, of course. Davey. Jimmie. And Keith.

His brother, showing them the way to Ben's lake.

Ross Colbourne. Davey. Jimmie. Keith. It was like a drum beat in his head, steel-toed boots on metal, a war-dance. Ross, Davey, Jimmie, Keith.

The *Frances* was sailing like a dream. "She will sail, Ben. Whatever happens to her in the end, she will sail." She was in the middle of the lake, out in the open. Anybody who looked would see her.

Ross Colbourne would look.

She'll never sail. Guarantee you she won't.

There was a scream rising in his head. He'd heard that before, too—the high, thin wail that came with the thundering boots. In the past two years he had learned not to let himself identify it. But now he knew what it was. Now he remembered where he had heard it first.

He had never heard Mom scream like that before.

Whatever happens to her in the end...

In the end, she had stopped screaming. There had been a bang, and the scream had stopped suddenly, cut short.

Ross got to the edge of the lake and stopped, holding his hand up. The other boys clustered behind him. Ross saw Ben. He saw the model. He grinned.

Melissa had warned him. "Look out to that dumb model of yours." But he hadn't, he had let her go free, and now she was out there, out in the open where he couldn't help her, sailing steadily toward the harbour he had once thought so safe for her.

There was no path around the long south finger of the lake; it would take forever to get to the harbour that way. And on the north side the enemy was between Ben and the harbour. He might swim across, but the *Frances* was sailing too fast; he couldn't hope to catch up to her before she got to the other side.

And the enemy would be there by then. They would take her out of the water before he could reach her. They would have her. His *Frances*.

When they had her, they would hurt her. It was what people like that did. They didn't have to have a reason. They just liked to hurt things.

"They pick on the strangers," the policeman said. "Somehow it's easier for them to justify. But if there weren't any strangers, they'd do it anyway. They seem to have to hurt."

It was the licence plate on the car that told them. A lonely car in an empty parking lot and a little kid inside, engrossed in your book and not even seeing them until they were right beside you...

"They don't read, themselves. And they see a little kid reading for pleasure and it's something they don't do and they don't like that. And maybe the little guy doesn't notice them right away, he's so caught up in his book. And that's not something they're used to and they don't like that, either."

What they didn't like they would stop, and they did. They got up on the hood of the car and kicked stars in the windshield and bellowed laughter and horrible words at you, and then when you were so scared you had made yourself into a ball on the floor of the car under the steering wheel and they still kept it up and their steel-toed feet were coming through the windows and in a minute they would unlock the door and hurt you, then you reached up through the bars of the steering wheel and you found the horn and you pressed it and pressed it and pressed it and you didn't think what would happen then or that it would be Mom who would run across the asphalt toward you. You didn't think that she would scream and scream at them to leave you alone and you could still hear her screaming even though the Giallar Horn was blowing and even though she was small and beautiful and had never hurt anything before in her life even though she was too little to do anything to help she was running to help you and they didn't like it and they stopped her screaming stopped her running stopped her stopped her stopped her.

Stopped her.

They went then. And you got out of the car and ran to Mom and she was lying on the black asphalt with her mouth wide open and something coming out of it a sound maybe a sound like the one you keep hearing now in your head somebody's making it and you can't stand it you have to stop it you have to—

"He's coming!"

One of the boys darted off.

"Get his model!"

They would hurt her. They had never stopped hurting her. They were hurting her now. He was in the car, the Giallar Horn blowing, but there was no way he was going to stay in the car this time, no way, no way. He howled—a sound, no words at all, a siren flying with him down the long white-hot tunnel between him and them, and only the end of the tunnel mattered, the bony, black silhouettes of the enemy at the other end.

And so he fell, ploughing headfirst through a bush into the end of the boardwalk. His breath whooshed out of him. Mud caked his eyes. His face burned. He lay there, flattened. For a long time he couldn't move at all.

And when he finally got himself up again and scraped the mud out of his eyes, the tunnel was gone, and so was *Frances*.

◆

Tor saw Ulf amid the press of howling coppery bodies in the clearing. He was leaning forward oddly, a big man but not so big now, not nearly as big as the tall Skraeling in front of him with a stone knife in each fist. It was Ovaegir, and he was nodding grimly. There was Northmen's blood on each stone blade.

Ulf tottered a moment, and then fell.

There was no time to think. A Skraeling was in front of Tor—he swung his shipbuilding axe, and something fell. Three more Skraelings broke through the space Ulf had left, slipped to the right past the bodies of Bjorn and Knut and headed at a run for the settlement. Was that a Northman's blade one of them held? Tor stared a little too long. "Behind you!" Nils panted. He dealt with that, and the one that followed, then got away somehow and raced through the forest to the settlement. As soon as the palisade came in sight his worst fears were realized. The gate was hacked open.

Three of them. And only Rollo inside to guard his lady and her little son. Gudrid, in Skraeling hands.

It was Tor who was her man, Tor who should have been protecting her. Heart thundering, he pounded into the compound.

FOURTEEN

*T*hey weren't in the longhouse. He had to step over Rollo's body to be sure. Gudrid, Snorri, the three Skraelings, none of them were there.

"Where?" Tor demanded of the weeping women.

They pointed to the doorway. "No," he said, "I would have seen them."

Astrid shook her head. "They were so fast," she whispered. "Rollo … took no time. And then they took Gudrid and Snorri. What could we do?"

Against three Skraelings who had killed an armed Northman in no time? "Nothing," Tor said, and ran back the way he had come.

He had seen nothing of the three Skraelings and their hostages on the cleared path between Leifsbudir and the lakes. They must have headed for the low-lying forest that blanketed the land everywhere the Northmen had not cleared. Once in the forest, they would be virtually impossible to trace. But eventually they must circle to the south to avoid the battle while still making for the *boggy shallows that lay between the two lakes above Leifsbudir and allowed the only quick route to the Skraeling encampment.*

It was certain that they would take Gudrid and Snorri to the encampment. Tor had to stop them before they got there. The tangle of forest would slow them. And Gudrid would do what she could to delay them even more. If he could get to the shallows before them…

He put on a burst of speed and headed down the twisting trail that led from Leifsbudir to the wooded knoll by the lake. The men had cleared this path through boggy scrub for the women to get to their cabbages. The Skraelings knew about the trail. Often they used it themselves. But the three with Gudrid and Snorri would not, because the trail led almost directly to the battle and they wouldn't want to risk Northmen seeing Gudrid and coming to her rescue.

Tor took the trail because it was the fastest way he knew to the water, and because from the high ground of the knoll he might catch sight of the three Skraelings and their hostages in the forest to the south. Then he would know if he had a chance, racing around the lake, to reach the shallows before them.

And if he did, well then, his job would begin.

Three against one. They hadn't been good odds for Rollo.

But Rollo was older than Tor, and not so quick. He couldn't have been alert, to have died so quickly. And Rollo wouldn't have had time to get angry.

Tor was already angry. Tor was very angry indeed.

◆

Ross and the others were down on the dock by the time Ben got to the viewing platform on top of the knoll. He saw them nudging each other and fooling with the *Frances*. Laughing. Only Keith looked up now and then, nervously.

Four against one. No wonder they were sure of themselves. And they had *Frances*, too. They thought Ben wouldn't attack them for fear they would do worse things to her.

But Ben had been down that road before. He had cowered in a car and done nothing and people had done the worst they possibly could anyway. He wasn't going to do nothing again.

The blinding rage was gone, wiped out by his fall. He felt very calm, precise as a machine, calculating odds, working out strategies. Four against one. But the four of them were on a dock. That was stupid of them. If the landward end could be blocked, they wouldn't be able to get away.

He chewed his lip. One against four. It wouldn't be easy to block the landward end.

But with a weapon...

He flattened himself against the hilltop and crept back to his Viking house. Was it still secret, or had Keith betrayed that as well? If he had, they would have messed up Ben's things. Ben pushed aside the juniper branch and dropped inside.

Everything was just as he had left it.

He got out the axe.

It was cold, icy cold, and heavy as a piece of lead. He hadn't really noticed the heaviness before. He hadn't noticed how sharp its blade was, either, or how bright. Even in the dim light of the longhouse it glittered. The linked rings decorating it seemed charged with fire.

It dragged at him when he climbed out onto the knoll. He held it two-handed, a murderous weight.

He scanned the lakeside. For a moment he was disoriented. It almost seemed as if there was forest along the knoll and between it and the path by the lake: thickly growing black spruce, tall firs, birch reaching white fingers into the sky. He shook aside his confusion. The enemy was what mattered, and they were where they had been before. He smiled. Open ground for them, cover for him. Good.

They thought they were safe.

The axe pulled him. Down the side of the knoll, fast, quiet. Into the trees. There was a wind, trees creaking and shivering, iron clashing on stone, screams. Open space now. The leader, still some distance back.

You got to him, that was all. You just stepped over everything in your way, and got to him.

◆

From the top of the knoll Tor could see knots of warriors colliding on the edge of the lake. The howls of men and the screams of the wounded were muffled by the dense growth on the sides of the knoll, but Tor knew that things were going a little too evenly for his comrades' liking. That was not his concern now. The quarry he sought would head south for the shallows. Desperately he scanned the forest in that direction. Nothing. Hardly daring to hope, he turned his gaze to the wooded bog that lay nearer to the trail between Leifsbudir and the knoll.

There. Movement in the brush—a flash of gold. The sun on Gudrid's hair? Far less to the south than he had expected, but... there! Again! He was sure this time. And only a score of boat-lengths away. They were taking a path that would hug the knoll and come out on the cleared lakeside to the south of the battle. They must have grown tired of the slow pace the forest imposed, and were going to chance the quickest route to the ford.

Tor hefted his axe and ran. He would be waiting on the lakeside when the enemy came out. He would defend his lady. He would make them pay for what they had done.

◆

"There he is! Ross, what're we gonna—?"

"Keep your pants on, my son." The tall one, that was; the leader. One-handed, he pushed the little one behind him and smiled. Yes, that was definitely the one to beat.

There was something in his other hand. He held it up enticingly. "Hey, big brother. Cute little toy we've got here.

Want a look?" He turned it upside down. Things clattered out.

"Don't hurt it." The little one, darting forward again, out of the leader's protection and clutching his arm. "Please, Ross, you said you wouldn't."

"That were before." He shook the thing in his hand. More clattering.

"Ross ..." Someone else.

"Shut it, Davey."

"But he's got a axe..."

"That what it is?" Sneering, but there were nerves behind the sneer.

The axe didn't feel heavy any more. The handle fit his palm. He hefted it, smiling. There were things you could do with an axe like this. You could wipe sneers off people's faces, for starters. You could take back what belonged to you. You could make people pay for what they had done.

Faces pressed to car windows. Five against one. Five, and a gun, against one.

With the axe, it was *you* people had to watch out for.

A measured step forward, smiling. Another.

The leader eyed him narrowly. "You got guts, I give ya that." He smiled, too. Then slowly, without changing the direction of his gaze, he bent and put down the thing he'd been holding in his hands. "But I got this," he said, erect again. He lifted his foot, then slammed it down, missing the thing by a hair. He lifted the foot again, threateningly. "All I gotta do is do that again, only different. Any bets who's gonna win?"

"Tor!" Gudrid cried. "Save my boy! Save—"

The Skraeling gripping her arm wrenched her to him, his stone blade at her throat. The second one held the baby under one arm, a knife in his other hand. The third was smiling, a blade in each hand.

You couldn't win, of course. Take even one step forward, just one, and the beautiful thing they had taken from you would be gone forever. Don't take that step, and they'd wreck her anyway, making you sit and watch. You'd been through it. You knew.

All you could do was make them pay a little. But after it was over, whether you made them pay or not, the ending would be the same, a thing you had loved lying dead in front of your eyes.

Ben gripped the axe berserker-style and swung it around his head in a futile attempt to find the rage he needed.

"Stop!"

Karlsefni's voice, rising above the battle. Everything went silent.

The three Skraelings were looking over their shoulders along the lakeshore. Even Gudrid was looking. Tor stepped back and sideways to get a view of what was happening.

Ovaegir had snatched a Northman's axe from one of his own Skraelings, who had clearly just killed with it. He stood there now, the axe high and dripping, his puzzled man beside him. Karlsefni was there too, hemmed in by Skraelings and obviously unarmed. In the middle of battle, with iron in his hands, Ovaegir stood with the axe frozen.

Ross still had one foot raised. Davey was on one side of him, Jimmie on the other. Keith hid behind. Ben faced them, three in a row with uncertain eyes in their grim faces.

Ross's foot would go down. Ben knew it. As soon as he went for them, Ross would slam his executioner's foot against *Frances*, smashing her into a million pieces.

But if he didn't go for them, it would be the parking lot all over again.

He had to do it.

Nothing moved except the whirling axe.

He had to do it *now*.

Ross's shirt suddenly jerked back against his chest. For the briefest of moments shock widened his eyes. Then, unbalanced by his upraised foot, he was flat on his back at the end of the dock. Everything was confused for a second, with Ross swearing and writhing and the other boys crowding around. During that moment, Keith scuttled out of the way, bent and scooped up something from the ground and ran straight to Ben, holding it out.

Frances.

"Here," Keith whispered, white with terror.

"Pulled me down, the little frigger," Ross exploded, down the dock.

"*Keith* did?"

"I'm gonna break his head."

Ben stared open-mouthed. Keith had saved *Frances* for him. He had attacked a boy four years older than himself, a boy he'd tagged after all summer, to stop him from destroying his hated brother's model ship. "Why?" Ben muttered.

Keith was crying. He couldn't say anything. He was still holding *Frances*.

Ben lowered the axe, taking one hand off it long enough to pull Keith around behind him where he would be safe. Ross was back on his feet. Davey and Jimmie flanked him ominously. "I need both hands for the axe," Ben told Keith, without moving his eyes off the three boys. "You take the model to our Viking house, and hide."

Keith didn't go. "Don't hurt them, Ben. Please, Ben. You've got your model back. Please."

Ovaegir stood frozen, the axe raised to eye-height. There were dead men all around, Skraeling bodies, Northmen's, the iron stink of blood. Karlsefni waited for the blow to fall.

Everyone waited for it.

Ovaegir looked at the axe he held, looked at the man he could kill with it. He shook his head. And then scornfully, proudly, he turned and threw the axe as far as he could out into the lake.

It was a killing weapon that far exceeded anything the Skraelings had ever possessed. It was for weapons such as this that they had fought in the first place. They were in the midst of battle even now. And Ovaegir had thrown it away.

Tor didn't understand it.

Ovaegir shouted something then, fully in charge and knowing it. His men stared at him. Then with their weapons brandished as carelessly as if their lives weren't in any danger, they began to walk past the Northmen they had just been fighting. One or two of Tor's comrades made as if to attack. "Let them go!" Karlsefni commanded. "It is a truce. Do not harm them. There will be other times for that."

Instinctively, Tor looked again for Gudrid. The Skraeling who had held his knife to her throat had just let her go. The one with the baby dropped him on the ground. In a moment Gudrid was on her knees cuddling the boy and whimpering. The baby was silent.

A part of Tor's brain went cold. Babies cried when they had been manhandled but were basically all right. And Snorri was not crying. The Skraelings had really hurt him, then.

The boy was in Tor's charge, and they had hurt him.

All three Skraelings were now walking down the lakeside toward Tor as if he were nothing to worry about, as if he and the axe he carried didn't even matter.

Karlsefni's truce had nothing to do with this. They had hurt the boy. Gudrid had prophesied that Tor would protect him, and he hadn't. It was his fault, and his duty to amend it.

And they marched on him as if they thought he would do nothing to stop them.

Shoulder to shoulder the three boys advanced on Ben, a

glitter-eyed saunter. They knew what to do in a fight, Ben could see. He laughed, oddly excited. *Frances* was out of their hands. Keith was on his side. The odds were getting better and better.

And there was no gun this time. He was the one with the weapon.

He swung the axe again. Round and round, faster and faster. It was heavy, again, but he whirled it anyway. It dripped.

This axe had killed Skraelings. Ben knew it, without knowing how he knew. It had killed, and it wanted to kill again.

And still the three Skraelings who had taken Gudrid walked toward Tor. He had his woodworking axe ready. He stepped into their path. Braced himself. They kept on coming.

It was then that the baby began to cry.

Tor's muscles trembled. Of its own accord, almost, the axe began to lower. But nothing changed on the faces of the three Skraelings. The baby was alive, and what did they care? They didn't even care that Tor had started to lower his weapon. They'd done what they wanted. They'd always do what they wanted, whoever got hurt. And they didn't think Tor or anyone else had the courage to stop them.

"He's not gonna use that thing, b'ys," Ross said. "You knows that, don't ya? A fight's one thing. Killing's different."

They knew about Florida. They knew Ben was the kind of person who hid in a car and didn't fight.

In the fog, on asphalt, blood looked black. It might have been oil, or water. But when you knelt in it, you knew.

She was still alive then. The gun was beside her. He had picked it up, closed his finger around the trigger, and pointed the gun to where they were disappearing into the fog. But she was whispering something. He had to bend over her lips to hear it. "Don't," she had said. "Please, Ben, please don't."

He had dropped the gun, hugged her, smoothed her hair back, made himself smile. "You'll be all right, Mom. You'll be all right."

"Remember. Remember what I said about Ragnarok. Only then, out of the dark..." She smiled drowsily, and then she died.

Round and round the axe whirled. Round and round and round.

Keith was plucking at his shirt, still crying. "Ben, please."

"Tor, no!" Gudrid's voice. "We are in truce. Don't avenge something that's already over."

Already over. Ben's arm slowed.

The worst thing that could ever happen to him had taken place two years ago in a foggy Florida parking lot. For two years he had lived in that fog, unaware that it was over.

"Only then, out of the dark, will life begin again."

It was the last thing Mom had ever said to him, and it was about life, not death.

The axe dropped to his side. For a moment he let it hang there limply. Then, with surprising force, he turned and threw it as far as he could out into the lake.

The three boys were farther back than they had been. There was something odd about their eyes. Ben said nothing at all, only waited. Behind him, Keith breathed raggedly.

At last Ross shoved his hands in his pockets, pursed his lips and shrugged. "Told ya, didn't I, Jimmie? He ain't doin' any killin'."

"You took my model," Ben said.

Time passed. Ross was silent. There was no clue in his face as to what he was thinking. The other boys waited.

Keith moved slowly out from behind Ben's back. *Frances* was still in his hands. "You said you wouldn't hurt it. You said you only wanted to look at it. You *said*, Ross."

"Anybody see me hurtin' anything?" Ross asked.

"You lost stuff out of it." Keith's voice was scared but defiant. "Oars and stuff. It's all over the dock."

"That right?" Ross chewed his lower lip thoughtfully. His eyes went to the dock. "Seems as if there might be a thing or two..." He bent slowly, picked something up. "Good bit of carving, that," he said, holding an oar out to Ben.

Davey bent over. "Here's a couple more." He picked them up.

"Bunch more here," Jimmie volunteered.

Three hands out, three hands offering. Hope filled Ben, hope and a kind of puzzled joy. Slowly he moved down the dock to meet them, Keith at his side, still holding *Frances*. Ross and the others moved forward, too.

They met halfway. One by one Ben put things back where they belonged. They all watched.

"You coulda used that axe," Ross said casually, after Ben was done. "Thought you would, for a while."

"I was mad," Ben said.

"Good little ship ya got there. Maybe we shoulda asked before we borrowed her."

Ben stood taller. "Want to see her sail?"

Ross looked at him from under his brows. Suddenly he grinned. "Okay, b'y, you wins. Keel like that, she's got no right to sail at all, but we all seen her. Not a trick, is it? She'll do it again?"

"I'll show you," Ben said. "Keith can help me." He looked at his brother. "She's called *Frances*."

"*Frances*," Keith whispered.

"It's a good name," Ben said. He looked at Ross. "It was my mother's."

"Always name ships after the women," Ross said. "After that, ya hafta make sure they stays off."

He grinned at Ben. After a minute Ben grinned back. Something swept out of him, out and away, something dark as a parking lot and heavy as an axe in mud. Lightness took its place. It was like sunlight pouring into him, golden and warm and lighting up all the darkness, it was like champagne, the heady bubbly stuff of New Year's, it was like a finished model and Dad making cocoa and Mom's voice telling the end of the Ragnarok story.

"There will be life and new life, life everywhere on earth. That was the end, and this is the beginning."

There was a book of gardening amid the shelves and shelves of books that Dad had bought for him. Mysteries, fantasies, fiction, and one solitary non-fiction book on gardening in a northern climate. Ben smiled. He would read them all, but he'd start on the one about gardening. It would be good to have a garden in their backyard. It would be good to have a tree—an ash tree, like Yggdrasill, growing tall and green on the edge of the sea to remind those who sailed these dangerous waters that there was safety nearby, if they needed it.

An ash wouldn't grow easily on Newfoundland's northern peninsula. An ash would need watching and care, protection from the things that would continually strive to destroy it. It would have to be looked after for a long time to become anything like Yggdrasill.

But he had a long time. He had ties to this place now. He had connections.

The Vikings had had to leave their homes. They had wanted to stay, but they had been forced to leave.

It had been Karlsefni's decision. "They will come again and again. We can never defeat them. We will return to Greenland in the spring."

Tor built no more ships. The last thing he made, a carved gable-head, Karlsefni sold to a Southerner for his own vastly dif-

ferent kind of ship. Sometimes when he was old Tor remembered that gable-head, sailing a Northman's sea on a Southerner's ship.

He had made the gable-head of maple from a land that these days none but the old believed even existed. Vinland, that they had had to leave; Vinland, that might have been their home.

The Vikings hadn't wanted to leave this place, but they had had to. Ben had wanted to leave, but now everything was different. Now he had a secret house of his own to share with Keith, and Melissa back in Ship Cove who'd be really and truly happy to see them all come back today as friends. He had Dad waiting for him in a house whose sunrise colours had something to say about people who made their homes in hard grey places. Most of all he had a Viking *Frances* of his own, his mother's *Frances*, whose home port would always be Skin Pond, Newfoundland.

Tor had gone away from here, but he, Ben, would stay.

And this time, he would make Vinland work.

AUTHOR'S NOTE

The Vikings did come to L'Anse aux Meadows in northern Newfoundland. Dr. Helge Ingstad was the archaeologist who discovered this fact. Though there is still a little controversy about whether or not L'Anse aux Meadows was actually Vinland (where almost a thousand years ago Leif the Lucky built the first European dwellings in the New World), most people now agree that enough artifacts and other evidence have been found there to prove that it was.

It's well worth reading the two different Norse sagas that deal with the settlement of Vinland—the *Graenlendinga Saga* and *Eirik's Saga*. These were both originally tales meant to be told rather than read, and they were not written down at all for a long time after they first became known. The tales changed over the years with different storytellers, and as a consequence, the people who eventually wrote down what we now think of as *The Vinland Sagas* had to piece things together, and the two sagas do not agree with each other on every detail. Where they differ, I used the account that seemed to me more convincing.

We know from the sagas that Leif didn't intend his houses of sod to form a permanent settlement. To him they were only a base for a winter of logging and fishing. He took back to Greenland a valuable cargo, on the way rescuing a shipwrecked woman named Gudrid, whose husband Thorir later died. Gudrid then married Leif's brother Thorstein, and when he, too, died, she married for the third and final time, an Icelandic merchant named Thorfinn Karlsefni.

Meanwhile, Leif's brother Thorvald had made his own

expedition to Leif's houses in Vinland, using them as a base for logging and for exploring the shoreline. According to the *Graenlendinga Saga* it was on one of his explorations that Thorvald came upon nine natives sleeping under their canoes. He named them "Skraelings" and ordered them all killed. One of them escaped, however, and returned later that night with more Skraelings to take their revenge. Thorvald was killed and buried in the New World.

The next Viking expedition was the first meant actually to colonize the New World. It was led by Karlsefni and Gudrid, who, according to the *Graenlendinga Saga*, brought sixty men and four other women to Leif's houses in Vinland. The settlers sowed seeds and kept livestock and had a favourable first year. Then they had their initial encounter with the Skraelings, who had come intending to trade, but were frightened by the Vikings' bull and sought shelter in the sod houses. Karlsefni had the doors barred against them. As the saga succinctly explains, neither side could understand the other's language. That lack of understanding was only to grow.

Eventually the Skraelings did establish trading relations with Karlsefni's settlement, but the Vikings got furs, and the Skraelings, milk. What the Skraelings really wanted was iron, because they couldn't forge it themselves (all their tools were of wood, stone and bone). But the Vikings wouldn't give it to them, or teach them the technology. Karlsefni believed that the Northmen's survival in Vinland rested on the superiority of their iron weapons, because they were vastly outnumbered by the Skraelings. It was a long Viking tradition to be more or less constantly at war with their neighbours, and so it probably never occurred to Karlsefni that an alternative to relying on weapons might be to live in peace with the Skraelings. He ordered a strong wooden palisade to be built around the houses. About that time his wife Gudrid gave birth to a son, Snorri, the first European child to be born in North America.

After the Skraelings discovered they were being given watered milk, real trouble erupted. A single Skraeling tried to steal the iron weapon he wanted, and was killed. The others fled, but Karlsefni knew they would be back.

He devised an ambush. Ten men made themselves conspicuous on the headland to draw the Skraelings to Karlsefni's chosen battleground, which had a lake on one side and the woods on another. Then, as the *Graenlendinga Saga* states,

Karlsefni's plan was put into effect, and the Skraelings came right to the place that Karlsefni had chosen for the battle. The fighting began, and many of the Skraelings were killed. There was one tall and handsome man among the Skraelings and Karlsefni reckoned that he must be their leader. One of the Skraelings had picked up an axe, and after examining it for a moment he swung it at a man standing beside him, who fell dead at once. The tall man then took hold of the axe, looked at it for a moment, and then threw it as far as he could out into the water. Then the Skraelings fled into the forest as fast as they could, and that was the end of the encounter. *

It would have been entirely possible for Karlsefni's ambush to have taken place near the knoll by Skin Pond. The area has changed a great deal in the last thousand years, from low-lying forest to present-day scrub and bog. If the ambush did take place there, it would have been Skin Pond into which the Skraeling leader threw the axe. Dr. Bob McGhee, an archaeologist who worked on some of the later excavations at L'Anse

---

**The Vinland Sagas, The Norse Discovery of America*, translated and with an introduction by Magnus Magnusson and Hermann Palsson, Penguin Books, London, 1965, page 67. Copyright Magnus Magnusson and Hermann Palsson, 1965. Reproduced by permission of Penguin Books Ltd.

aux Meadows, confirmed that if the axe had gone into Skin Pond it would probably still be more or less intact after all this time because of the preservative properties of the peat mud at the bottom of bog-lakes. Further, he was enthusiastic enough about the idea that the axe of the saga might have been thrown into either Skin Pond or Black Duck Pond to tell me he'd like to go out there and look for it himself. After that, I felt quite comfortable about having Ben find the axe, and use it as he did.

It was after the Skraeling leader threw the axe into the lake that Karlsefni decided to give up his dream of colonizing Vinland. The settlers returned to Greenland the following spring.

There was probably one further expedition to Vinland, made by Leif's half-sister Freydis. (The two sagas differ greatly in their reports of this. In the *Graenlendinga Saga* Freydis is said to have made her expedition after Karlsefni's; in *Eirik's Saga* she was supposed to have gone with Karlsefni.) In any case, Freydis's expedition was marred by greed and envy among the Vikings and, depending on which saga you believe, ended murderously or merely unpleasantly.

After this, there are no further recorded Viking expeditions to Vinland.

All the geographical places mentioned in *Out of the Dark* are real and recorded as accurately as my notes and research and memory allowed, though in Ship Cove the locations of my characters' houses are invented. Quarterdeck Cove is real and quite lovely, though it is not named on any map I was able to discover. I was told its name by a local guide, who explained how and when he would take his family there by boat. The knoll by Skin Pond exists, as does Ben's Viking house. So do his rock and his harbour, though I would be very surprised— and delighted!—if you found the *Frances* moored there or sailing from one side of the lake to the other.

There is indeed a miniature lighthouse village in Ship Cove, which was, I was told, made by a teenaged boy who has since moved away. Although I got to know quite a few of the people in Ship Cove, none of the present-day characters in *Out of the Dark* are based on real people, living or dead. Of the historical characters, only the ones mentioned in the sagas actually existed. This means that Ben's Tor did not come to Vinland with Karlsefni and Gudrid, though I agree with Ben that he ought to have.

I rendered the Norse myths as faithfully as I could while allowing myself to emphasize the things in them that I thought would be of most importance to Ben. The most fascinatingly connected retelling of the Norse myths I've ever encountered is in Roger Lancelyn Green's *Myths of the Norsemen* (Penguin Books, 1960). Perhaps the most beautifully rendered is *Axe-Age, Wolf-Age* by Kevin Crossley-Holland (Faber and Faber, 1988).

L'Anse aux Meadows was designated a World Heritage Site by the Unesco World Heritage Committee in 1978. A plaque erected on the site states: "L'Anse aux Meadows is the first authenticated Norse site in North America. Its sod buildings are thus the earliest known European structures on this continent; its smithy, the site of the first known iron working in the New World; the site itself the scene of the first contacts between native Americans and Europeans. It is therefore one of the world's major archaeological sites."

It is a site I fell in love with before I ever went there—years ago, when I first read about it. I have been to L'Anse aux Meadows now, and I love it even more. I, like Ben, can feel the Vikings there. And I, like Ben, wish that this Vinland had worked out better for the Vikings. I also wish it had worked out better for the so-called "Skraelings"—a word which in the Viking tongue meant "uncivilized wretches"—who in the end learned the cost of what they thought they wanted, and had the powerfully civilized good judgement to throw it away.

DATE DUE